THE COUNTERFEIT HEINLEIN

THE COUNTERFEIT HEINLEIN

Laurence M. Janifer

WILDSIDE PRESS
BERKELEY HEIGHTS NEW JERSEY

THE COUNTERFEIT HEINLEIN

Wildside Press
PO Box 45
Gillette, NJ 07933-0045
www.wildsidepress.com

First Wildside Press edition: March 2001

This adventure is
for my dearest treasure,
who dislikes to see
her name in print.

ONE

THERE WAS ONCE something called science-fiction. (I know, I know, there is now, but it's not the same—this was preSpace.) It began more than a hundred years before the Clean Slate War, and for a while it concentrated on what it kept calling exciting stories of science—look at all the wonders today's mad scientists are going to bring us any decade now, that sort of thing. There was a Julius Verne, for instance—some of his things have survived, but not *20,000 Leagues Under the Sea*, which irritates me; I've always wondered how many of those Leagues were red-headed, like the one in Sherlock Holmes. And there was *The Foot of the Gods* by Herbert Wells, which also hasn't survived (although *War of the Worlds* did, and is actually fairly exciting, if you can get hold of a copy somewhere).

But science-fiction started to change; things do. It began to concentrate more on people and on ideas (it was a commonplace of the time to say that science-fiction was a literature of ideas, though I am damned if I can imagine anything else for a literature to be of), while the detailed science surrendered the steering wheel and slowly slid into the back seat.

Just a little while after that, science-fiction began to deal in matters that were scientific only by the most haphazard of definitions—everything from parapsychology (not just telepathy; telepathy exists, but this was something else again), a charming superstition a few especially wishful ancients thought of as psychology, and eventually such things as witchcraft, numerology and the Great Beyond.

And then . . . well, you get the idea. After the Clean Slate War, when enough pieces had been picked up and shoved back together, there began to be science-fiction again, but it had very little to do with science—any more than a great many comic-books or comic-tapes have to do with comedy.

Now, there are people who know all this in great detail, or in as great detail as the surviving, and often confusing, records allow. (Was there really an author named Spider Callahan? Alfred Blishter?) I know it in fits and starts, because I did have a scrappy sort of Classical education once upon a time, and some of it has stuck. More, I took the quick course, so to speak, when Ping first mentioned his job to me; I collected all the information I could get at, and three or four sorts I hadn't really thought I could get at until I tried.

That, after all, is what a Survivor does—that's what it says on my business cards: *Gerald Knave, Survivor*—in spite of what you're used to seeing on your 3V. Up there, a Survivor is a grim, wordless sort of hero with a hot beamer in each hand and a great willingness to kill off half the cast on no very special provocation.

A Survivor, and I'm sorry to shatter such illusions as you may be harboring, is essentially an information collector. You never know, in my trade, just which bit of information you are going to need in the Hell of a hurry, but you do know that, when the red signal lights up, you are not going to have the time to find it. Therefore, you gather in everything available, as long beforehand as you can manage, and you keep gathering in more information, more or less all the time.

This particular job—Ping's job, for which I read up on my preSpace sf, as it was called—actually began rather suddenly, and pre-Ping, with someone taking a shot at me.

There I was, sitting quietly in a leased apartment on Ravenal—where I had gone to hobnob with some of the friends I have in high places—drinking coffee out of a china cup, watching my rented Totum direct two rented Robbies in the fine points of apartment-cleaning, and trying to decide which of several interesting restaurants I was going to invite Jamie Arthur to, later that evening. The coffee was Sumatra Mandheling, which Ravenal imports for a few discerning Nobels and suchlike. The time was fifteen-eleven, City Two local time; Ravenal has a twenty-four hour day, almost exactly, and even a twelve-month year. I take my coffee with cream and sugar, not in excessive amounts.

Well, how did I know which fact might be the important one? It was a coolish late-Spring day, and I had my window open, and just at fifteen-eleven (which I am always going to think of as three-eleven P. M., since I do not have the Scientific Mind) something went *whizz-crash-tinkle*, and my lap was full of hot coffee. I was holding the cup's handle; the rest of the china had left it, to complicate the apartment-cleaning situation.

I sprang up with many an eager curse, dropping the handle and dabbing at my pants with both hands. In something under a full second, sanity returned, and I dropped to the floor, where I lay with my face in the luxurious carpet for ten full minutes. The Totum directed the Robbies to clean around me, not over me; Ravenal's rental machines, as one would expect, are fairly bright.

Any sensible marksman, I kept telling myself angrily, having missed the first shot by a reasonably thick hair, would have potted me in that endless second before I dropped. I kept muttering that into the damn carpet while I waited. For ten solid minutes. Of course it's not especially helpful to set time limits on a marksman's patience when you have no idea who the Hell he is, but ten minutes seemed about right as a wild guess, even adding in a safety factor.

So I struggled upward, let my machines get on with their work, and didn't get shot at again.

And nothing else of vital importance happened that day or that night. Jamie and I had a pleasant dinner and a pleasant few hours of chat (I'd finally chosen an "old-fashioned British pub" with surprisingly good food, if all too predictable atmosphere—the name had at the least a definitely ancient feel: the Rose & Corona).

I did not, just by the way, spend my time waiting nervously to get shot at again. My hopeful assassin had had his one shot, and he hadn't taken any more. It seemed unlikely that he'd be bucketing around all over City Two (that's Ravenal for you: extraordinarily bright and accomplished people, with no literary imagination whatever—not even Twin City or Doubleville) angling for another try.

No, I relaxed and enjoyed myself, and Jamie seemed to enjoy himself, and I went to bed in a calm and fairly peaceful mood.

I did make quite certain to shut and lock all the nice, unbreakable-glassex windows.

And the next day at ten-thirty—somebody had asked round about me, and discovered that I keep civilized hours—the telephone rang, and it was Ping, whom I'd never so much as heard of before, offering me a job.

* * *

HIS NAME WAS Ping Boom, and I am not making that up—my God, who would? It is amazing, if not downright sickening, what some parents will do to saddle their offspring with lifelong jeers and scars. Admittedly Boom is a surname that does cry out for ridicule, but would Abraham Boom, or Callian Boom, get quite the reaction I gave Ping Boom when he told me who he was? I doubt it.

But when I was persuaded that he wasn't trying to spoof me somehow, he turned out to be a very businesslike fellow. I agreed to meet him after I'd treated myself to a lovely, hand-crafted small breakfast, and, nicely cleaned up, was in his office by noon, or noon-thirty. "We want you to do a very specific job for us, Knave," he said. He was a short, thin fellow with sparse whitish hair, large, ancient-looking eyeglasses, and a mouth that was better than halfway toward Pursed Disapproval.

I told him to specify away.

"We want you to find a missing manuscript. It's quite valueless, but enormously important."

I asked him, as calmly as possible, just how that combination worked out; at first glance, it seemed just a trifle odd.

"It's a forgery," he said. "A counterfeit. It purports to be the work of a preSpace writer named Robert Heinlein."

I'd known more than the average reader about Heinlein even then–my Classical schooling–and he wasn't quite preSpace; when the first moon landing was made (by Armstrong and Harriman, I believe) Heinlein had still been alive.

"If it's a forgery," I said in a reasonable tone, "then why is it valuable?"

"We can't yet determine just how the forgery was managed," he said. "It's so nearly a perfect counterfeit that it fooled our experts for over four years–and our experts, Knave, know their business. Or businesses, of course."

We were, after all, on Ravenal, home of the Ravenal Scholarte (where Ping Boom was co-chief librarian, Manuscript Division). I agreed that Ravenal's experts knew their businesses; they always do.

"So you want me to track down the manuscript," I said.

"Exactly," Ping Boom said. "It's been stolen–very neatly, too. There's been some talent at work here."

We discussed some other matters–payment, for instance. I won't bother you with the whining and screaming on both sides, so common in such discussions, but we finally managed to arrive at a mutually unsatisfactory figure, and I agreed to come down and take a look at the scene of the crime, as the first step in finding the missing non-Heinlein.

"There's nothing to see, Knave," Ping Boom told me.

"That's exactly what I want to look at," I said, and we settled on a time.

TWO

THE LIBRARY OF Ravenal Scholarte (more Nobels per square cerebrum than anywhere else in the universe), or the part of it I went to visit, was a large and very odd building, about six or seven standard stories high, the usual perches on two big windows per floor, and the general feel of a museum. Many of Ravenal's public buildings are fairly showy—the place tends to substitute tradition for imagination—and in the library they had a fair imitation of the ancient Grand Central Station, sitting, unfortunately, exactly in the middle of a sizable square of space planted with greenflower, and (as in the old joke) much larger. Grand Central Library, as I christened it (the Scholarte called it First Files Building) seemed to own something on the order of a hundred entrances, each leading into a maze of echoing corridors lined with doors. The doors looked like velvet-bordered wood—a nice, expensive touch; it's not on the regular settings—but weren't really there, of course; they were the usual hologram shows covering lock-and-unlock fields. Technologically, Ravenal is a bit more up-to-date than the date; half the improvements in the known systems seem to start there. I waited for Ping to unlock the Special Exhibits door, halfway down the hall on the left, and followed him inside.

Everything was laid out under actual glass. "We try to fit the period," Ping whispered to me, and I wondered just how he'd present, say, any bits of the Dead Sea Scrolls. I nodded, and we tiptoed around for a few minutes, getting accustomed to the glass and to the lighting.

Glass isn't glassex—it's transparent and it comes in sheets, but it has a shine to it that just isn't there for glassex. The wildly old-fashioned fluorescents that lit the room did not mate nicely with the glass; glare was everywhere, and your head had to be at one of a few particular angles for you to see inside the manuscript cases.

But they were worth the effort. There was a notebook—one of the Future History notebooks, and open to a page on the ancestry of "Andrew

'Slipstick' Libby." In Heinlein's own handwriting–a decisive, clear written hand, not at all the sort of scribble one associates with mid-Twentieth holographs.

There was a printed copy of *The Man Who Sold the Moon*, the original Shasta edition–some collector back before the Clean Slate War had had the remarkable good sense to bag it and either put it in vacuum or get caught in his own shelter airlock with it when the war began. The case was sealed ("Argon atmosphere," Ping whispered), but I thought, romantically and inaccurately, that I could smell the original, actual paper and boards and glue.

There was a manuscript copy of a very early Heinlein–"And He Built A Crooked House"–also in a sealed case, of course–and there was a disk that contained, according to the case label, a few of his headnotes for his final collection–that one has been lost, damn it–and a job lot of personal letters.

And there was more. I won't tantalize you with it–except to mention a color photograph (long faded, and almost as long restored) of Robert and his wife Virginia, taken, according to the label, somewhere in California at some time between 1960 and 1972.

Of course, California is more mythical today than Heinlein–at least some of Heinlein has survived. The little 2D photo got to me, somehow, and I was dabbing at my eyes, just a bit, when I turned away from it. Ping nodded.

"It does seem to affect people that way," he said, and I told him it was the dust in the room. He nodded again and we let it go.

At last I tore myself away from the damn precious relics, and asked: "Where was the forgery?"

"The manuscript that was stolen?" Ping said. "Over by the window," and he walked me over past a row of cases to a big window–glass like all the rest in the 20th-C wing, shining into my eyes very disturbingly–that looked out on a grove of trees. Maple, I thought, and those things from Rigel IV–walking-trees, the ones that used to stampede. I was sure of the walking-trees, since I'd been the one who had put an end to the stampedes.

Long, long ago . . . it was a shock to realize how long ago, and the odd thought gave me a very distant feeling of kinship with Robert Anson Heinlein, of much longer ago.

A few steps before we reached the window, Ping stopped at an empty space just big enough to fit a case. "We haven't yet replaced it with anything," he said. "A late-Twentieth word-processor keyboard, perhaps, with its own attachments, just to give the feel . . ."

I agreed that would be nice, and asked after the case the manuscript had been in. Ping looked at me in surprise.

"Oh, that," he said. "The Pigs have it."

It took me a few seconds. "The police?"

He nodded, looking a little shamefaced. "One does get carried away," he said. "I become so late-Twentieth in here . . ."

"I'll have to see that case," I said. "Carefully and extensively. I'll have to have some other people see it."

"I'm sure the–the police will be reasonable," he said. It was more than I was; in my experience the sort of people who choose policing as a career are also the sort of people who are only as reasonable as they absolutely have to be.

"You'll have to tell them I'm officially in your employ," I said. "Otherwise, I'm just some Joe from Kokomo."

Ping stared. "Some what from where?" he said.

"Slang," I said. "Somewhere in the Twentieth, probably pre-Heinlein."

"Ah," he said, and nodded again. It was one of his strong points. "To be sure. I'll speak to the police. Anything else, Knave?"

"I want this room sealed off," I said. "It's probably too late–when was the theft?"

"Two days ago," he said, and I stifled a curse. Well, the police would have a lot of details, and perhaps they really could be persuaded to share.

On the other hand, I was going to have to take their word for all those details, many of them now long gone. I have, as it happens, a strong dislike for taking anyone's word, at any time or place, but my own–but there was no help for it on this job. I was arriving late, the first-act curtain had gone down, and as Act II started I was going to have to do the best I could with my printed program and whatever help I could tease out from the other spectators.

"One more thing," I said, concluding that I'd also get a better picture of the actual mechanics of the theft from the police, and tucking away sixty or seventy questions for them, later on. "Who handles Berigot assignments for this floor?"

"B'russ'r B'dige," he said, and I filed the name away. He was certainly around the building—it was nearly two in the afternoon (fourteen, if you have the Scientific Mind), the building was open, he'd be working—and I could locate him through Berigot Services for the library. I wished Ping a polite good-afternoon, took one last look around at the priceless collection—I like Heinlein, however many fashionable people tell me he's dated—and walked away, heading toward Berigot Services.

And it occurs to me just here that you might not even know what the Berigot are. We'd better get that in first, because we're going to need it.

THREE

EVERYTHING IN THE universe looks like something we already know, even when it acts very differently—which may be a statement about the universe, and may be a statement about the way we know things. Walking-trees look like trees, though they're not, and the Berigot—

Well, when you tell someone they're a race of sailplaners, for some reason the immediate reaction is Bats, and you start hearing a lot about Dracula and other ancients. The Berigot don't act like bats (except that they do flock—but even people flock), and they don't look like bats—they look like giant flying squirrels. They're large, and they're furry rather than, say, hairy, and their arms do look fairly small and fragile for the size of a Beri. Their heads even seem to be pouched, although the shape isn't due to a pouch system but to twin air-bladders; that's how they speak. The whole breathing system is reserved for breathing.

The wingspan is very large, of course, though even so they can't really fly. They walk at times, with a whole range of mincing gaits that look as though they ought to be very painful, and they swoop and dip at times—they prefer swooping and dipping, and so would I, but that sort of thing needs height and clear space, which are not always available. At home, they live in what some people call nests and other people call perches, and use the ground for large storage buildings; at work they enter and leave from perches set high enough from the ground to allow of some sailplaning.

They come from a planet called Denderus (their name for it; humanity has politely agreed to stick with it, since humanity can pronounce it), which has a Standard gravity of .89, and air as thick as, say, Earth's—this is possible because the stuff isn't air, it's a denser set of compounds. The Berigot can't breathe our air, and sensibly don't try; even if you have seen a Beri or two, you've never seen one without his transparent head-bubble. The exchange technique isn't quite beyond human skill, but it is said that only four men on Ravenal, and perhaps two more elsewhere, understand how the bubbles transform Ravenal's air into stuff a Beri can breathe.

There's a small human presence on Denderus, and an equally small Berigot presence in the Comity Worlds, almost all either on Earth where the diplomats live or on Ravenal, where the Berigot have found appropriate work. They are probably the best librarians in the galaxy (Kelans might dispute this, but the Kelans aren't much on really big libraries, preferring to carry their massive knowledge around inside their rather small heads).

People do tend to think of a librarian as someone who will direct you to the spools for Non-human Dance Troupes, and who spends a staggering proportion of his time saying *Shhh.* This is not quite the whole picture; librarians are a vitally important part of any search for knowledge, though virtually nobody knows this except other librarians, and a scattering of searchers.

I know it because I have had to search for some odd things now and again, in the course of an active life. Ravenal knows it because the Ravenal Scholarte and all its associated cities are always searching, though they seldom have any clear idea of what they're searching for; if they knew, they'd already have it.

And Berigot know it because collecting facts is what Berigot do.

I've said a little while ago that a Survivor—me, for instance—is first of all an information collector, and as an information collector, I'm fairly good—for a human being. For a Beri, I would be classified as Deeply, even Laughably Defective. The Beri collect information the way human beings invent weapons—with constancy, facility and blinding speed. They would make me feel horribly inferior—if they did anything else.

Oh, they eat and sleep and mate (four sexes, two He and two She, all needed not only for reproduction but for a normal social life), but their reproductive (and social) life is passionless and managed pretty well by rote, they have no hobbies except those associated with information-collecting, and they have only very recently begun to wonder whether there is anything in the world at all *except* information-collecting. Human beings are the bit of information that has started them wondering, and Ravenal has contributed most heavily, since Ravenal is the sample of humanity a Beri is most likely to see.

Someone on Ravenal, about seventy years ago, awoke to the fact that a race of information-collectors would make marvelous librarians, and began talks with the Berigot. And the Berigot have been working on Ravenal ever since.

Well, what does a librarian do, except point you at the spools you need, or tell you to *shhh?*

He—and if the pronoun has been irritating you, I'm afraid you'll just have to be irritated; it's all I can do, and I'm robbing the Berigot of two pronouns as it is—he puts one piece of information together with another piece of information.

I've heard of that process as the one absolute definition of intelligence. I agree: the ability to take two facts and make a third fact is intelligence, and everything else is something else. Unfortunately, it would take either the Kelans or an even brighter race to come up with a useful test for it.

But the Berigot are very good at it. It's what librarians do: they look into Non-Human Dance Troupes for a bit, and remember something they noticed the last time they looked into Molar Physics a bit, and they see that the two things have some common features.

Then they tell people about this—either personally or, much more frequently, by filing a cross-index note. Molar physicists can now get a bit of help from non-human dance troupes, and vice versa.

This goes on all the time, in fields even more widely separated than my examples. Librarians are the great cross-pollinators of the universe, and they make things grow—things like ideas, and inventions, and discoveries, and civilizations.

Ravenal, naturally, has the best librarians known. And I was off to see one.

I'd met a few Berigot, on a previous stopover, but for me the meetings had just been a few minutes of casual chatter. For a Beri nothing is casual (which means that nothing is important, either; if you don't have a scale, you don't have a top to it), and I felt sure somebody would remember me—though possibly not at Berigot Services, which is staffed by human beings.

Services greeted me as a total stranger, and called Ping to check on me. They're a deeply suspicious bunch, and they should be; five years ago, Ravenal (just about five and a third, Standard), according to report, some nut decided to get dangerous, and tried shooting at Berigot. He made a nice, if somewhat ragged, hole in each of three Berigot–in each case puncturing some part of the strong webbing with which a Beri sailplanes; only natural, as it's the biggest target in flight, and all three were hit while off the ground.

Police built up a fair picture of the nut, who had been using an unfashionable, but very damaging, slug gun, and their final working theory was, believe it or not, that he'd been a sports maniac, and had decided the Berigot were fair game, like ducks or some such. They'd never managed to snare him, despite some helpful data (by Berigot, of course, who notice things), and since that little series of incidents Berigot Services has been just a hair paranoid.

The Berigot themselves take things more calmly; their feeling seems to be that nuts happen, the way earthquakes and economic depressions happen, and one has to get on with life.

So when I knocked on the door of the Frontier Worlds History room, B'russ'r B'dige simply unlocked the field and poked his head out to see who'd come along.

"Gerald Knave," I said.

"My goodness," he said. His voice was clear, with a slight echo, and a little high even for Berigot, who tend to the tenor ranges. "I know of you, Knave. Have you come to add to my knowledge? Come in, please come right in."

"I've come to borrow from it," I said. "I'm here about the Heinlein manuscript."

B'russ'r smiled. Berigot have rather pinched, open smiles, and they look more pleasant than my description does. "Ah, Heinlein," he said. "'What are the facts? Again and again and again–what are the facts? You pilot always into an unknown future; facts are your single clue.' Our attitude exactly, Knave."

He stepped aside and I went in, and he closed the field firmly behind me.

"Now, then," he said. "A phrase, by the way, whose oddity has always appealed to me–now, then–well, what do you want to know?"

I found a chair and sat down. B'russ'r remained standing, of course, his legs locked; a Beri can't sit and doesn't want to. I took out a cigarette (Inoson Smoking Pleasure Tubes, Guaranteed Harmless–no Earth tobaccos—but most people do seem to call them cigarettes) and offered him one. He nodded and took one and stuck it through his head-bubble (I'd had no idea it passed Inoson Smoking Pleasure Tubes as well as sight and sound) into his mouth. "I have never understood why humans burn these things," he said, and began to chew, slowly. "I don't think I have ever seen cigarettes dyed red before, Knave."

I explained that I had them made, lit mine while B'russ'r found a handsome ashtray—map of the Ravenal Scholarte pressed between glassex panels, in gold—and explained matters to him. He grew very grave, munching away at his cigarette.

"Someone should have been on duty," he said. "Someone should have taken notice."

"Notice of what?" I said. B'russ'r shook his head.

"Of the actual theft," he said. "The process itself—it must have taken appreciable time, after all."

"Now that's what I want to know," I said. "How was it managed? What do you know?"

"Know? Very little," he said. He was still chewing thoughtfully. Apparently Berigot don't spit. "We have some deductions, and the police have told us of a very few—ah—clues."

I asked for a consecutive story first, and then got down to details and went back and forth. I made notes as we went along, and B'russ'r watched me do that with a curious resignation. When I asked him why, he said: "We use a better method: upload data directly to the nervous system, as non-sensory input, for classification and filing. Automatic, but humans somehow won't take to it."

"I wonder why not?" I said, not even wanting to think about shoving megabytes of strange data into my nervous system.

"I think it must be the loading system," he said. "It is bulky, but we found room by shrinking parts of our reproductive systems. I'm sure humans could do that."

"Well," I said, smiling with some effort, "maybe they will. Some day." A dedicated race, the Berigot.

FOUR

THE ROBBERY HAD taken place, as all good robberies should, at dark of night. The thief or thieves (and there was a general consensus that there'd been a small crew) had somehow a) managed to get across the grounds of the building, not easy because the place was sub-electronically guarded–a pulsating field (a look every twentieth of a second) from three feet below ground to six feet above–and b) managed to get through into the room where the manuscript had been on display, and remove it. The thing had still been on display–the forgery wasn't quite public knowledge, though not hard to find out about, and the forged manuscript was to have been removed and stored under Curiosae two days later.

Getting into the room had been quite a trick. The windows were locked from the inside (real and very old-fashioned window-locks, late-Twentieth in style but newly made of real metals). There was a Berigot perch nearby, but what difference it made nobody could see, since, if you somehow managed to get to it and onto it from the ground, you were still looking at the locked windows. Nothing had been broken. There were no fingerprints, no meaningful residual heat-spots, on the windows themselves. There were residual heat-spots on the inner sills, and on the floor leading to the case–as good as footprints, and showing two or just possibly three human people, the small crew already mentioned–and the case itself had been wiped clean of everything including heat by an alcohol mixture. The locks on the case showed signs of tampering.

I asked B'russ'r: "Now, why would you expect someone to have noticed?"

"Even late at night," he said, "there are Berigot in flight. We enjoy to fly, and require the exercise. There were none on this side of the building–we will have to see about arranging our exercise flights with more care."

"Not your fault," I said. B'russ'r nodded.

"I know that, Knave," he said. "It is not fault I consider. But someone should have noticed." He did what Berigot think of as a disapproving motion; both small arms twitched forward under the webbing. "There must have been noise, even if faint. The alarm should have gone off."

"Apparently not," I said. "These three, or however many, slipped through the alarm like ghosts. Through the window, too. Not a trace anywhere."

"And the case showed signs of tampering," he said. He swallowed twice. The cigarette was gone. Mine had long been ash and a small red remainder, in the glassex ashtray. "No trace at the window. Definite traces at the case. Does this dichotomy suggest anything to you?

I shrugged. "Insanity, possibly. Little else."

"Nor to me," he said. "But it must mean something. It is too odd to be meaningless."

I thought about lighting a second cigarette, out of sheer frustration, and decided I didn't want to see B'russ'r consume another one. "You have good instincts," I said.

He smiled again. "They are not instincts," he said. "They are consequences of information upload."

"Whatever you say," I told him, wondering idly what such a thing meant. Deduction from known facts? Echoes of gigabytes in the nervous system? "I'll need you to talk to some other people, by the way. Within a day or so."

B'russ'r nodded and smiled. "Of course," he said. "Master Higsbee, and I should think little Robbin Tress."

I stared at him. Those names were notions in my head, and nowhere else. I had mentioned neither of them to Ping, or to anyone else. I had seen I would need help with this job, and I'd thought of asking the Master and Robbin. Only thought of it.

Berigot were not, as far as was known, telepathic. It would be the Hell of a secret for them to keep.

"How do you arrive at those names?" I said after several silent seconds.

One more smile. A friendly smile. "A consequence of information upload," B'russ'r said. "I know of you—an amount about you. I know of many people on Ravenal. I said to myself: other people? The choices seemed predictable. It took me some time."

His response had been instantaneous. "I am impressed," I said. I swallowed. Hard. "You will talk to them?"

"Of course," B'russ'r said, and positively beamed at me. "Who knows what I may learn from actually meeting them?"

God knows I didn't. I said my farewells–Berigot don't shake hands, and it is better so, but we hissed politely at each other, and tilted heads in opposite directions–he left, I right.

After that I went to see the police, who were much less unsettling.

FIVE

THEY WERE ALSO less informative. They did open a bag or two out of their hoard on the case, but none of the bags contained anything I could think of any way to use. They had a few flakes of dried skin from a bit of floor near the case–people shed, and few beings outside police labs know it–but they'd been too small and too trampled to provide anything much in the way of data. They had the beginnings of a typing on the dried skin, just enough to limit the suspects to fifty-five million. With great good luck and much work, perhaps fifty-three million.

After a while I left, feeling just a bit lost, and thoroughly inferior until I remembered that B'russ'r, certainly, had also had a chance at the police files, and had got no more help from them than I had.

I was heading back to my rooms, to call the Master and get him to call Robbin–unless one is one of three people in the universe, one does not call Robbin. I was on a main boulevard, nicely tree-lined (maple again) and uncrowded. The time was eighteen-seventeen, or sensibly 6:17 P. M. I was not smoking, muttering or whistling, and I was wearing nothing unusual. I did need a haircut, and had for a few days.

The slug hit the sidewalk less than a foot behind me. This time there was no hesitation; I leapt as if cued for the building line and dropped flat there, bruising my nose, one shoulder and both knees. I didn't know about the bruises until some time later; I was much too busy listening and, as far as my position allowed, looking–though I neither saw nor heard anything helpful.

A few passers-by stopped to help me. I lay still until I had collected a small crowd of hesitant Samaritans ("Don't move him, you don't know what's wrong"), and then allowed them to raise me up, dust me off and help me to a nearby shop. I stayed in the middle of the crowd until well inside the shop, which sold portable walls.

A nice portable wall sounded like a fine idea, but I didn't really have time, and even if pressed couldn't carry one everywhere; people would talk.

Four or five Samaritans had given the shop-keeper the story of my rescue, very variously, and I sank down on a small chair over by one (permanent) wall and breathed for a little while.

Ten minutes, in fact. It might have been eleven. In either case, I'd given my assassin more room than I had before, because all that Samaritan-collecting had taken time.

Then I stood up, and thanked the wallman, and walked out into the early-evening light. It took me another ten minutes to amble on home, during which time nothing of any interest happened to me.

And, once home, I made completely sure every unbreakable glassex window was shut and locked, told the Totum to take itself and both Robbies to somewhere restful until called for, dressed my small wounds a little, and got to the phone. Voice only, image available for some extra button-pushing and a nice steep charge, but I was not looking my best, and forwent it.

I hadn't spoken to Master Higsbee in five years, and it was a delight, in a way, to hear that rasp of his again—a sound like an unoiled camshaft with attitude. The phone rang twice (on Ravenal, by the way, it doesn't ring—for some reason, it blips) and a voice said: "Who?"

It is no damn way to answer the phone, and never will be. "Knave," I said. "Hello, Master. How are you?"

"Ah, Gerald," he said. No one else in the entire Galactic collection of vocal races calls me Gerald. I think I dislike it. "A long time. And how should I be? An old blind man, helpless and alone, in a world made for the sighted and the fleet—Gerald, how should I be?"

I sighed a little. The Master would always be the Master, after all. "You'll be fine," I said. "You always are."

A snort from the unoiled camshaft. "By dint of unceasing effort, Gerald, I remain alive and—so far as I may—functioning. In sixty-one months Standard, what have you done?"

I took his word for the time; one could. And I knew what he meant. "Not much, Master," I said. "I did learn how to lockpick a hologram safe, and I've had a few liaisons."

"Children may result from the liaisons, one cannot be wholly sure," he said. "Good. The lockpick is too simple for you, Gerald—you must stretch yourself."

I refrained from saying that I'd stretched myself quite a lot in some of the liaisons. When talking to Master Higsbee, one lets the Master make the jokes.

"I'll look round for other things," I said.

He sighed. A cross between a wheeze and a derby-muted trumpet. "Well, enough," he said. "What have you called to demand of an old man?"

"I've got a problem," I said, and Master Higsbee said at once:

"The Heinlein forgery, of course. What do you need of me?"

There are days when I am not at speed with the entire rest of the universe. This never feels comfortable. "You've heard about the theft," I said.

"I have," the unoiled camshaft told me. "Gerald, put out the cigarette. The smoke does not of course come through this connection, but the signal of it, your changes in breathing, discomfits me."

I stubbed out the Inoson Smoking Pleasure T. Why could I not need someone else?

Because, damn it, there *wasn't* anyone else. Not like the Master. "I need a full consult," I said. "Examination of scene, questioning of some people. Everything. And a running consult with me on all aspects–all but one."

"You will handle one aspect alone, Gerald?" he said. "If so, which one?"

"Not alone," I said, and he said:

"I will call her in–sixty-three minutes. The soonest possible. She will then call you."

"Direct? Herself?" I said. "Robbin has changed."

"Improved, they think," he said. "To some degree."

I nodded at the phone. I was not wholly sure the Master couldn't detect that in some way. Changes in pressure, perhaps. The sound of my head moving in the air. After a second I said: "I'll be waiting. We'll arrange a meeting after you've both been around the block on this. I'll give Robbin names and places–writing them down will give her something to do, and she can tell you, giving her something more."

"You are learning, Gerald," he said. Distant approval. I seldom got anything that warm and cozy from the Master. "When we spoke last, you would not have thought of that."

"Thanks," I said. I wanted to ask him once again if he were still sure he would not have his eyes restored, and decided against it. It would be badgering, a very bad thing.

"I will call you when we have—been around the block, Gerald, and we will all meet. It has been good to hear from you. Finished."

The connection broke. I sighed yet again and put the phone away, and made myself a cheese sandwich (eight minutes) and a pot of coffee (twenty-two minutes, and worth it). I ate, drank, washed the dishes, and did a little light dusting while I waited for the phone to ring. There are times when I am just too busied, too frantic or too damned lazy, but, most days and weeks, I do my own housekeeping. It's a bit like a hobby—restful, and a way to free the mind while the body occupies itself. Home or away, any Totum and Robbies I have around are just a tad underworked, I think. They don't complain of it.

Forty-eight minutes later, dustrag stored away and an edge of boredom starting to set in, the phone rang. I got it on the first blip, and there she was, or her voice anyhow, after sixty-one months Standard, the Master's figures, the usual breathless childish soprano bleat.

"Hello there, thank you so much for thinking of me, Sir, do you want me to help with your work? Master Higsbee says you do."

I was always rethinking it, but I felt just then that I liked Sir a few hairs less than Gerald. "I do want your help, Robbin," I said. "Do you know the situation, love?"

Robbin was thirty-two Standard years old. At times she very nearly looked as old as twenty. At times she very nearly acted as old as eighteen, but not often. "Of course I do, Master Higsbee told me about it," she said. "We were on the phone for a *long* time." She giggled. I don't get to hear giggles very much, and prefer my life so arranged. "Sometimes I think he *likes* me," Robbin Tress said in her teeny breathless voice.

"Well, good, I'm sure he does," I said. The girl could reduce me to babbling banality in any twenty-second space of time. "Then you know you're to take down names and places?"

"My pen is right here, Sir, all ready." I gave her a list, from B'russ'r B'dige through Ping Boom (she giggled) to a few police officers male and female. The Master, I knew without thinking about it, was going to have to interview the females, and try to get Robbin what she needed from them.

And the few important places as far as I knew them: the room where the manuscript had been, the lawn outside, the Berigot perches for that building. There would of course be more. I had the sudden lost feeling you get when you've forgotten something important, and added just in time my apartment and the stretch of street near the portable-wall shop. "Do you want me to see your apartment while you're in it?" the breathless little voice asked.

I stared at the phone. "Do you do that now?" I said.

"Sometimes," Robbin said. "For people I know a long time. The Master would have to come too, though, if you don't mind, Sir."

I nodded, and then said: "Fine. When?"

"An hour and a half, Sir?" she said. "I will call him, and then wait for him here."

Robbin had improved out of all belief. "An hour and a half," I said, and began to give her directions.

"Oh, Sir, don't bother about that, please don't trouble yourself," the breathless voice said. "The Master will know, he'll take me. Closed car, Sir, I really have done it before."

"Fine," I said. "I'll see you both then."

"Goodbye, Sir," Robbin said, "and thank you so much again for thinking of me."

Finished. It might be that the Master's way of ending a phone talk had a point. I said goodbye politely, put the phone away and thought about refreshments. Coffee of course. And–

I had time for one fairly speedy shopping trip. Nobody shot at me.

SIX

AND THIRTY-FIVE minutes after I came back weary and heavy laden, as the Bible says, there they were, actually sitting in my living-room. The Master took his coffee black. Robbin Tress took hers with cream and sugar, as I did, and if something as small as that could have made me doubt the habits of a lifetime, little Robbin's taste in coffee would have. I'd settled on a sort of local fruit-cake, sticks of hard cinnamon bread, a few cheeses, and some fruit, which turned out to be a mistake: plums, from what were advertised as actual descendants of actual Earth plum trees. They might have been—who am I to argue with advertising?—but if so, a great deal had happened to the family in the intervening centuries, all of it terrible.

Robbin was delighted by the exotic plums, which didn't make up for the look that crossed Master Higsbee's face when he bit into one. But the cake was good, the cheeses acceptable, and the coffee Indigo Hill, the emperor of coffees, from my own stock. And the talk rapidly became helpful.

"The first question, of course," the Master said while refilling his cup, "was why the forgery had not been detected earlier. This is, after all, Ravenal. These people can be expected to know their business, and indeed they usually do. One notes the occasional exception, but one does not note many."

"Maybe it just cost too much to find out," Robbin said dreamily. I remembered just in time not to object, or to wonder where she'd gotten such a notion from. "Dreamily" was the key, of course; Robbin in that sort of tone was being Robbin.

A long time ago, back when there was real science-fiction, there was also a place called Boston, which was supposed to be stiff with tradition of several sorts. Maybe it was—at this distance how can anybody tell tradition from random habit? At any rate, the traditional Boston ladies, if that's what they were, wore some perfectly terrible traditional Boston hats, and one day (according to an old story) somebody asked one such lady where she got her hats.

"In Boston," she said, "we do not get our hats. We *have* our hats."

Robbin did not get her ideas. She *had* her ideas. I had once described my two guests to an interested lovely to whom I was spinning a tale, and hoping for Othello's satisfactions, if you remember (and there is no good reason why you should): if my lovely would only love me for the dangers I had passed, I was more than willing to love her in return, for she did pity them. Master Higsbee (I told the lovely, who was indeed fascinated, and if not wholly loving toward me, certainly in frenzied like) knew everything that could possibly be known. (That was perhaps just a touch exaggerated. Not really very much.) Robbin Tress knew the things that couldn't possibly be known.

The people on Cub IV, where she'd been born and, so far as the phrase was applicable, brought up, looked on her as a sort of wild psi talent, and on Cub IV, where there'd been a history of difficulty—open damned warfare, in fact—with psi talents among non-humans, this did not make her popular. How much of little Robbin's personality was originally built in by manufacturer, and how much was the result of social strain—to put it very, very mildly—during her childhood and teener years, nobody may ever know, though small dedicated crews on Ravenal do keep trying to find out. What she has doesn't seem to be psi, exactly—it doesn't follow any of the normal rules for such things, even where there are any rules. Robbin doesn't seem to know anything she isn't asked about, or somehow prodded by interest into thinking of. And she doesn't reach the answer by any process anybody has ever been able to understand; the answer isn't reached at all; it is simply going to be there. As closely as anybody has ever been able to see, if you don't ask the question (or otherwise engage her interest), the knowledge isn't going to be there; if you do, it is. Maybe.

When word of Robbin got to Ravenal (as word of most oddities does seem to, sooner or later) a state of fascination ensued, and after a little backing and filling (and not very much) Robbin had a new home, and many new friends. People who did, in fact, actually like her, and did their level best every minute not only to solve the set of very frustrating puzzles she presented, but to help her.

Which was why Robbin Tress was on Ravenal when I needed her.

Master Higsbee was on Ravenal, of course, because where else would a man who knew everything knowable be?

And both, as I say, were being helpful. Master Higsbee nodded when Robbin mentioned the high cost of finding out about the forgery, and told me:

"In fact that was the reason, Gerald. The normal tests were run. Isotope assay was conducted on the paper and the ink for carbon-14, and for some quicker decay isotopes. A full run on all checkable isotopes simply represented too much of an expense on a very, very slight chance."

"The chance being that somebody had figured out a way to beat some isotope patterns, but not others," I said. The Master gave me a faint nod. I was doing well.

"Exactly," he said. "As far as was known, isotope assay was infallible even in limited form. Why, then, not simply agree that assaying some distributions would be enough?"

"And it wasn't," I said.

"A friend of yours, Gerald, is a great admirer of Heinlein. He is also a thorough man, and it worried him that a thorough job had not been done. He contributed his own funds, in part, for a full assay, persuading First Files Building to pay the remainder. And the forgery became obvious."

"A friend?" I said.

I have never heard anybody give Mac's name the way the Master did. "Charles MacDougal," he said. Apparently he really is immune to a lot of normal human itches.

It's a name most people want to shake full out, like a flag: Charles Hutson Bellemand MacDougal, B. S., M. S., Ph. D., this, that, and the other, full Professor of Molar and Molecular Physics, Ravenal Scholarte, a holder of two Nobels and, I am happy to admit, an old friend. I've heard people say C. H. B. MacDougal, and I've heard a lot say Mac. But Charles MacDougal was a first that night, and has remained an only. In fact it took me about two seconds to figure out who the Hell the Master was talking about—I was as dislocated as I'd once been when a Professor of Ancient Literature, years ago in my boyhood, mentioned Francis Fitzgerald instead of F. Scott.

"Mac was involved in this?"

"'Mac' was the cause of the forgery's being discovered," he told me testily. A little testily. "In fact, I have now said that twice."

Robbin said suddenly, and dreamily, breaking the Master's irritated mood: "They counted all the isotopes, and some of the numbers didn't add up right." Which is an inelegant sort of way of describing what had certainly happened.

The ancients knew about isotope assay, in a typically-ancient, half-hearted fashion. Carbon-14 dating, well known before the Clean Slate War, is an isotope-assay process: you see what percentage of carbon atoms in your sample are carbon-14, and you know (within limits) how long the sample has been around, because carbon atoms decay from carbon-14 to carbon-12 at a known rate.

By now the process has been extended to very small sample numbers of virtually every isotope possible in nature (or created by that most unnatural product of nature, Humanity, before, during and after the Clean Slate War), and it is possible to pin down a date for a physical object pretty closely—lots of isotopes disappear more rapidly than carbon-14 does. But the process is still expensive, and every element has to be assayed separately. Some day we'll have a simple one-step snapshot process, but probably not, I am told, within the next century.

A one-step snapshot would have identified the forgery instantly. As it was, identification had to wait four years, for Mac's worries to happen. But it was absolutely certain: isotope assay is not a horseback guess.

Robbin was finishing off the fruit cake piece by piece—the woman has the metabolism of a forest fire, and when in the mood eats large restaurants out of house and home without even blurring that sticklike figure of hers—and looked up from her digestion to ask one question of her own. Robbin does ask questions, not so much because she wants to know answers, but because she likes being told stories. And this felt to her like a good one.

"How was the manuscript supposed to have been found, anyhow? I mean, not who forged it and everything like that, we don't know that yet, do we? But what did somebody *say* happened?"

She was right. It was the Hell of a good story.

SEVEN

IT SEEMS THERE was a man named Norman W. Nechs. In fact there probably was–it seemed simpler even at that point to assume a real Norman W. Nechs, and a story for the forgery grafted onto him, than to assume that the forgers had invented and built the entire structure. And the assumption turned out to be good; there had been such a fellow.

Norman was alive during the ancient days, before the Clean Slate War. He lived in a state then called Uta, and what he did to make his living we do not really know. He may have been a State Patrolman, and according to the experts there are signs that he was, though there are stronger signs that he was a dentist, as we'll see–and if we only knew what a State Patrolman was or did, in the State of Uta, we would be much further along in making Norman's acquaintance. We do know what a dentist was, and did, and it sounds perfectly awful.

As it is, what we know for certain about him is that he liked science-fiction.

Remember, this was back in the days when there really was such a thing–when the giants like Benford and Sturgeon and all the Smiths were alive and actually writing all those wonderful stories we don't have any more, and a very few we do. Norman undoubtedly liked, and disliked, and felt strongly about, a thousand other things, like everybody else at any time, but what we remember now is that he liked science-fiction–and was something of a Survivalist.

Survivalists were not some primitive incarnation of Survivors. I don't have much in common with Norman, not that way. We share an affection for Heinlein (apparently he really did like Heinlein, but then most sensible people do), but not much more.

A Survivor is a person who goes out to survive on a new planet, mostly, in order to prove that it can be done by a wave of willing, if less capable, colonists. Bringing the fight to the enemy, so to speak. A Survivalist was a person who'd had the fight brought to him, and who was trying, every passive way he knew how, to live through it.

"Passive" is the key. Your Survivalist didn't go out to do battle with the things that were threatening his survival. That's what *I* do. What a Survivalist did was take one deep breath, tell himself those things could not possibly be fought, and try to figure out a way of living through them.

All the ways Survivalists did think up involved digging immense holes in the ground, surrounding them with armor of every available sort, making sure nothing could get in to the eventual armored space (air was allowed in only when cleaned, taken apart and put back together), and stocking that space with everything you were going to need to continue living—food, water, video games, spare pajamas. Everything. For periods of up to ten or twelve years.

That is Earth years. Comity Standard years. A Survivalist was a person who was determined to live in an armored hole in the ground for three times as long as it takes the light of Proxima Centauri to reach him on Earth Twelve years.

Most of these people, naturally, were crazy. A few did survive, came out of their holes ten or twelve years after the Clean Slate War, and were more or less immediately wiped out by natural processes; in ten years most germs and viruses mutate. Few of them had much stamina left in any case; some had rigged exercise spaces in their holes, but none had continued grimly exercising for ten years, and it is hard to imagine any human being who would. And all were ten to twelve years older, something few had apparently figured out would happen in ten to twelve years. Many had jungled up, so to speak, at, say, 40. These people came tottering out at a prematurely aged 50-or-above. The rest of humanity—such of it as was left, and of course there were people left, protected from immediate blast and radiation and firestorm by any six of a thousand possible accidents—living out of a fallout pattern, surviving the two to three years of truly Biblical weather—this rest of humanity sometimes killed them, and sometimes tried to help them. A few Survivalists lived as long as seven years after coming out of their holes. One, male, is recorded to have had a child by some woman less particular than most; survivors didn't much want to mate with Survivalists, feeling that insanity was not a welcome part of the gene pool.

Were there other ways of surviving? Survivors proved there were. And a little simple thought would have given some answers. Take all the money that was sunk into one hole-in-the-ground after another, barrel it up, and fund a research program with it. Take your pick of research objectives, active or passive: a) Go after the causes of such insane behavior as the Clean Slate War was clearly going to be, or b) build real and functioning force fields.

But the ancients, though full to the bung with the learning we now call Classical, were not really very accomplished at simple thought. Instead, they had luck—which accounted for survivors of the Clean Slate War—and Survivalists—which didn't, much.

Our Norman was a Survivalist. He had died in his armored hole. We now think he had had a heart attack, after having lived down there for about two years. I think I might have had one, or an attack of something, possibly suicide, after less time than that. Nor was this the end of his troubles.

His air-machinery was temperature- and humidity-controlled, of course. The humidity control went out about three months after Norman died. The air became very, very dry.

When the pie was opened—nearly three hundred years later, because Uta, whatever it was back then, is a fairly isolated place now, and though there are always archaeological search teams, there are not all that many, nor are they all that well-funded—when the pie was opened, there was Norman, dry as a mummy and almost as well preserved. And there were his artifacts, also fairly well preserved, considering, by the unlivable climate inside Norman's armored hole—though he'd tried, with some success, to do some extra preserving of some artifacts. Not sensibly—that would have been too much to ask of Norman W. Nechs, or probably of any Survivalist—but with great, even showy, dedication.

One of those artifacts, according to the discoverers, was a manuscript, nicely sealed in a mostly-nitrogen atmosphere, in a large, vacuum-sealed barrel of sorts, by Robert Anson Heinlein. It was entitled *The Stone Pillow.*

EIGHT

WORD GOT OUT very, very quickly. There are a lot of Heinlein fans, whatever fashionable critics say, and a high percentage of them know about *The Stone Pillow.* It is one of the unwritten stories of Heinlein's Future History. If you know about this, you can skip the next few paragraphs, and pick things up at the space, or the beep, or the sunburst, however you're getting this report. For the others:

Unwritten, anyhow, until Norman's carefully preserved manuscript turned up in his armored hole. There were three stories listed in old charts of the Future History that had never been written–*The Sound of His Wings, The Stone Pillow* and *Word Edgewise*–but apparently Heinlein had actually written at least the middle one. Why it had never been published nobody knew, and the suggestion that it was too lousy for publication was never made. It was, after all, Heinlein, and "too lousy" did not occur. Even "lousy" occurred only once or twice in the entire Collected Works, as far as we know today, and there is not much agreement about where, or even whether, to paste that label.

The Future History–well, there were a lot of these, though Heinlein's may have been the first, not only before the Clean Slate War but before World War II, which takes us all the way into antiquity. None were accurate, but accuracy was never the point— the point was to create a framework to put stories in, so that the stories meant a little more all together than they could one at a time. World-building, which is what a lot of science-fiction seems to have been, takes place in three dimensions of space and one of time, and Future Histories use up the time dimension most thoroughly.

In Heinlein's, there was a period in which the United States, his model for society, fell into a dark age, under the rule of a religious crank called the Prophet, Nehemiah Scudder. *The Stone Pillow* was supposed to tell the story of some of the rebels and martyrs fighting Scudder and his successors, and that was all anybody knew about it until Norman's little keepsake turned up.

It turned out to be the story of Duncan BenDurrell, a convert to the fighting faith of Diaspora Judaism and second-in-command of a religio-political rebel army fighting the current Prophet, third of that title, in a wild and uncitified area of what was, in Heinlein's own time, Oregon.

* * *

It was at that point, as I was spinning all this out for little Robbin Tress, that the Master interrupted me.

"You have never actually seen the manuscript you speak of, have you, Gerald?" he said in that rasp of his.

I shook my head.

"Let me, then, recite a brief passage," he said. "It was really a remarkable forgery, in its way—this will show you why, very briefly. Quite typical of early-middle Heinlein, and quite persuasive."

Robbin was sitting wide-eyed, one bite of cake held forgotten between two fingers. I felt that way myself—forgery or not, I felt as if I were going to get a quick glimpse of a Heinlein story I had never read before. I had to remind myself to start breathing again, at least long enough to say: "Sure. Go ahead."

Even Master Higsbee's rasp of a voice couldn't spoil the effects. I'll give it to you straight, though—the way it would have looked in print, starting (I checked, much later) with page 94 of the manuscript.

* * *

94

believe a word of it. But he frowned angrily, and he thought he looked fairly convincing doing it. He owed that much to the Dias, and he delivered it.

"That may be so," Joshua said. "But whatever you think of him, you must admit Duncan has been acting suspiciously."

"I'll admit no such thing," Frad said. "Duncan BenDurrell may not be an honorable man—as you and I understand honor, Excellency—but that's no cause for suspicion. The Prophet Himself tells us that there are not sufficient honorable men in an entire city to save it from destruction, though only ten be needed. Discourses, 3:13."

Joshua stirred uneasily, swinging a leg as he shifted a little on the rickety Judgment Seat. "I say BenDurrell—and the name alone stinks in an honest man's nose—is in league with destruction, friend Frad. And I say destruction should be his portion, as the Prophet suggests for unbelievers—Originations 4:10."

Outside the Summer Palace, a group of celebrators began to shout songs and hymns as they wove drunkenly past. Frad felt it wise to throw a glance of irritation at the open window, and Joshua shook his head and clucked disapproval.

"Such displays should be coventried," he said, and Frad shook his own head. It was possible, he knew, safely to disagree on such a point.

"Do not attempt to be more pious than the Prophet himself requires," he said. "It is said that all men need at times to unbend—Discourses 2:2—and who are we to judge their lives? BenDurrell is of an unfortunate heritage, Excellency, but that is all that can reasonably be said against him."

"We are appointed to judge," Joshua said mildly.

"So? Who was it made the appointment, Excellency?"

Joshua smiled. "God has made it," he said serenely. "God, through His First Prophet and through that Prophet's successors. What would you, then?"

"I will not pick a quarrel with Him," Frad said, "nor His First Prophet, nor that First Prophet's successors either. But it has never been clear to me that the proof of such an assertion is beyond any cavil."

"Then search yourself until you find that clarity," Joshua said, and a hint of sternness came into his voice. "You sail too close to the wind of heresy, Frad Golden."

Frad shrugged. "It's of no importance," he said. "But, in these difficult times, we must avoid even the appearance of injustice."

Joshua stirred a little on the Judgment Seat. "No one will worry about appearances, Frad Golden," he said. "BenDurrell is nothing, less than nothing. No one will bother himself over one man's fate."

"But BenDurrell is just that, Excellency," Frad said, as gently as possible. Joshua might listen to reason—the possibility existed—but it would not do to anger him. Duncan would not be well served by the casting-out or imprisonment of Frad Golden.

"'Just that'? He is nothing, and less than nothing."

"He is one man, Excellency, as you have said," Frad went on. "And like every man, he is the one for whom the First Prophet came, as He Himself said—Generations 7:33. He is the one for whom sacrifices were made, in the days of the beginning. We are taught that every man has such value that he, alone, might be the cause of all the work of the First Prophet, and all the mercies of God Himself. One man, Lord—as valuable as any one man in all this world. As valuable, one might say—so we are taught, an you read it aright—as the Prophet himself."

NINE

WHEN THE MASTER'S rasp stopped, the place was very quiet. Little Robbin Tress whispered: "Wow. Gee, Master Higsbee–gee, Sir–wow, I wish it were real. I mean I wish it were a real Heinlein story." And then, dreamily: "Maybe, someplace, it is."

"It might be so," the Master said. His voice sounded tired, but no more tired than usual. If asked, he'd have told you, extensively, how worn and ancient he was, and how much the recital had taken out of him. So I didn't ask.

Robbin offered to help with cleaning up, but the Master knew how I feel about household chores generally and dishwashing in particular,. and managed to persuade her that my refusal was serious, and not ill-tempered in the least. We spent a few minutes in reminiscence–Robbin had once been a help about a Fairy Godfrog, of all the damned things, and the Master remembered some odd consulting he'd done for me here and there (and all the reasons why I shouldn't have had to consult him, but could very well have figured matters out on my own)–and then, with both parties readying graceful goodbyes, it happened again.

This time, the damn nuisance didn't miss.

Of course, this time he wasn't shooting at me. In fact, we none of us heard the shot, for which I was and am profoundly grateful; that one sound would have tossed Robbin back five years and more in her own progress, and, which seemed almost as important somehow, would have been the occasion for endless complaining from Master Higsbee.

Six or seven minutes later, we were finishing up goodbye-and-reply routines, of which Robbin had a full set (the Master's version was of course short and simple) when my phone blipped, and they stood frozen at the door, the way people will, while I went and answered it.

B'russ'r B'dige's sweet high tenor asked me if I were me, and on getting confirmation gave me the news. I said I would be right the Hell there, hung up, and began to shoo my guests out before I had a chance to think.

Then I stopped shooing them, and instead began telling them what had happened. "That was B'russ'r B'dige. Somebody has just shot Ramsay Leake and knocked him off his tenth-floor balcony. B'russ'r thinks it's connected. I'm going down to the Leake place—want to come along?"

The Master took one quick look at Robbin Tress. "I think not, Gerald," he said slowly. "We will have to catch up later—of course you will provide. But Robbin should be home."

The girl was absolutely crestfallen. She was actually wringing her hands, something I don't seem to see much. "I'm so sorry, Sir," she told me earnestly. "But it is a strain, and they tell me I have to be careful about strain. In a little while when I'm better, I won't have to be so careful maybe, but right now I do, Sir, and I am sorry but I think I do have to go home, if Master Higsbee will help me get there."

She did have enough spirit left, or something, to bat her eyelids at the Master a little, and stifle a small giggle. To his credit, he let both pass as friends, not even asking for recognition codes.

"Of course," I said. "I'll check in with one of you as soon as I can, and as soon as I know anything. But let's shut up shop in a hurry—I'd like to get there while the scene is still a scene."

The Master nodded. Robbin was still agreeing we should hurry when he bundled her into their waiting closed car and took off, and by that time I was flagging a passing taxi and giving him directions to VT.

Which was, of course, the name of Ramsay Leake's modest estate—Leake being a computer-simulations expert. If you don't recognize the allusion, that's because it *is* rather a Classical tag; back before the Clean Slate War, computer people on early comm networks used to speak of RT and VT—Real Time, or life every day, everywhere, and Virtual Time, or life on the comm net. The differences were beginning to be appreciated, apparently, right from the start of comm networking, and Leake had reached back to the ancients for his estate name, as a neat enough challenge to those differences, and one I found instantly admirable. Unfortunately, I couldn't compliment him on it, not any more.

He was right there—what was left of him. But there wasn't enough left to compliment—after a ten-story fall, there was barely enough left to recognize. Ravenal has 0.97 Standard gravity, but the 0.03 difference didn't seem to amount to much in practical terms just then; Leake was just as jellied by the impact as he'd have been if he'd come down somewhere in ancient Oregon, or Uta.

VT had been a ten-story tower, round and rather thin, sticking straight up and surrounded by terrace-railings every two stories from the fourth on up. The word that sprang to mind, out of ancient literature, was "minaret". A fascinating building, and about one hundred times as imaginative as your average Ravenal structure of any sort at all. Oh, why not—a thousand times. Easily.

B'russ'r was there, too, some distance from the minaret, chatting politely with a police official I'd met briefly, a Detective-Major Hyman Gross. I climbed out of my taxi and ambled over to join them, perhaps thirty feet from the body, where a small army of techs was at work taking photographs, measurements, readings and anything else not nailed down. As I came within earshot, Gross was saying: "I respect your abilities. Hell, anybody respects your abilities, Mr. B'dige. But this isn't even a large coincidence. Sort of thing that happens all the damn time, I mean to say."

B'russ'r only nodded at the man patiently.

"It is not the coincidence of the weapon that concerns me," he said. "It is the coincidence of the occupation—not, I think you will agree, a small matter. My conclusion is a consequence—"

"Of information upload, I know," I said. "Hello, B'russ'r. Major Gross."

The Major gave me a stare. For Gross, this was a large undertaking: he had a red round face, even redder up where most of his hair had once been, and big, big eyes that bugged out as far as I've ever seen a human being's. He focused those exopthalmic things on me and said: "You too, Knave? What is this now, a plot? Are you ganging up on me now?" in a wheezy, wine-soaked little baritone.

"Perhaps Knave appreciates the situation," B'russ'r said.

"I might," I put in, "if I knew what it was. Leake fell from his tenth-floor balcony. How in the name of the original preSpace Gross do you know he was shot first? The shape he's in, that ought to take a careful autopsy."

"The shot was seen and heard," B'russ'r said. "This time, we have witnesses."

Gross snorted. "What do you mean, this time?" he said. "If you truly want to tie this death here to the Berigot shootings five years ago, you had a job lot of witnesses then. We all of us did."

B'russ'r stirred his wings a bit, forth and back. Confusion, and enlightenment–the Berigot equivalent of Aha. "I see," he said. "There has been a misunderstanding. It is not the shootings I wish to connect, Major Gross. It is the theft."

"Theft?" Gross said. "And just by the way, Knave, who the Hell is this 'original preSpace Gross'? Relative of yours? Some long-forgot relative of mine, perhaps?"

B'russ'r nodded a little sidewise at me, and I shrugged. Translated: "Do you mind if I supply the data?" "Not at all, go right ahead." Berigot are very polite, even a tad ritualistic, about information transfer. Naturally, I suppose.

"The Gross referred to," he told the Major, "is the author of *Modern Criminal Investigation*, a much-used police textbook just preSpace. Not only historically noted, but at times still quite helpful; his differentiation of some burned corpses from fight victims remains classic." He bowed just a trifle. "Not perhaps a subject of study in today's academies," he said. "As for the theft–"

He went on to describe, very sketchily, the Heinlein-forgery situation. Gross nodded. "And you believe this death here is connected?" he said at last. "Why? What would connect this Leake with an old manuscript?"

"Leake," B'russ'r said, "would have helped to fake it. The conclusion is, if not certain, surely irresistible."

Gross said: "Why would you say irresistible? Why would you come to any conclusion at all, for heaven's sake? Look, Mr. B'dige, you mention occupations. Well, this Leake was a computer-simulations expert. Whatever your old manuscript might be, it wasn't a computer simulation. When it was written new, perhaps there were people who didn't even have computers."

B'russ'r cleared his throat–something a Beri never does, except to imitate humans. I'd been wondering when he'd get around to it, and now he had. "B'russ'r, please," he told Gross. "It is true that B'dige is a name. But like most names placed in second position, for Berigot, it is functional, not personal. Simply B'russ'r, please."

"Not personal?" Gross said.

I nodded sidewise at B'russ'r, and he shrugged back at me. "That second name," I told Gross, "is a little bit like 'Teacher,' say, or 'Driver'—and a little bit like 'redhead' or 'shorty.' It describes a function or an attribute of some sort, not a person. The name a Beri uses is his *name*—the first part. The second part is more of a title, or a nickname—at nay rate, functional, not personal."

Gross nodded. I have no idea to this day whether he'd got it. But he did say: "Good for it, then: B'russ'r. All right with you?" and B'russ'r nodded very politely.

"Thank you," he said. "And as for your question—the manuscript was, in a way, a computer simulation. Such a simulation must have been used to create the effect of the forgery; at the detailed level at which it was constructed, there would be no other way."

I'd had the taxi ride over to think that out, and of course it made sense. Gross hadn't had either my additional minutes, or B'russ'r's information upload, and just looked confused.

"Some of the isotope assay checked out," I said. "And how do you build a pile of paper, and a barrel of ink, that has an isotope percentage match to, say, 1950 instead of 2300? You do it by running the entire molecular makeup through computer simulation, tracking it back in time, and coming up with a simulation giving you just the percentages you need for 1950. Then you make the 1950 recipe into a 1950-plus-350-years recipe—more simulation work—and build the paper from that. Done completely, it would be undetectable, because every isotope assay would check out. Why it wasn't done completely, we don't know. Apparently even the forger can't manage that yet."

B'russ'r rustled his wings, spreading them open just a bit and then shutting them, two or three times. Applause. "Flawless," he murmured. I bowed just a trifle.

"There's a job lot of computer-simulation experts, now," Gross said. "It's not as if this Leake person was going to be the only one in the galaxy. Or even the only one in the whole of City Two."

"The forgery was stolen three nights ago," B'russ'r said quietly. "Leake was shot dead tonight. This would call for rather a large coincidence."

Gross snorted again. "Coincidences do happen, B'russ'r," he said, and B'russ'r nodded, and said just before I could:

"So they do. Connected events also happen. One must learn to distinguish."

At which point a tall thin woman in a tweed suit bustled up to Gross and said: "We're done here except for final temp comparisons and assay. Okay for the M. E. to take him?"

Gross opened his mouth, sighed and shut it again. He turned to B'russ'r. "Would that be all right with you, now?" he said.

B'russ'r bowed politely. "Thank you for asking," he said, just as if Gross had had any choice; once a Beri was there as consult, even self-called as B'russ'r clearly had been, he had official standing. Berigot *noticed* things—and had no prejudices. "Knave is of official standing as well. If all right for him, it is all right for me."

Gross turned a little redder. "Wonderful, then," he said. "Just wonderful. Knave, how is it for you? I mean to say, now: may we go ahead and do our work?"

"Go right ahead," I said. "You have my cheerful permission."

TEN

WHILE THE POLICE were bustling around removing the remains and making sure everything not nailed down had been photographed, measured, assayed or bagged, B'russ'r filled me in. Leake, it seemed, had been standing on his top terrace, apparently just relaxing at the end of a long virtual day, and some distance away a couple of Berigot had been sailplaning at the end of their real-world ones. One of them caught the muzzle flash of a handgun, and heard the sound—a slug gun of some sort. Within less than a second Leake had staggered back, taken a couple of shuffling steps forward with one arm out and the other hand grabbing at his chest or stomach, and pitched over the terrace rail. The two Berigot, who had started to fly to him at the first stagger, split; one went on to try to help the body on the ground, while the other landed immediately, some distance off, and called police—before joining his companion at the murder site.

I filled B'russ'r in, too. When he heard that I'd been shot at twice, he sucked in air, or what passes for air with a Beri, and looked shocked. "You told no one of this?" he said. "And there was no investigation?"

For a change, I was able to explain to him something he should have known. "If I'd started telling officials, I'd never have got rid of the officials," I said. "I'd have had bodyguards, watchdogs, God alone knows what. Each one of which, at every second, would have stopped me from looking around and finding out something. And each one of which would have scared off the gun, and made him that much harder to locate."

B'russ'r nodded. "And of course there were no investigations—no witnesses. The first in your rooms, the second on a street, and all anyone knew about that was that you fell down and had to be helped to a shop."

"Exactly," I said. Well, I'd managed to explain part of it before he did, anyhow. "But if there were any remaining doubt about the connection, we can now lay it to rest for good."

Another nod. “I should think so,” he said. “In all cases a slug gun. Not the usual weapon, though not truly bizarre.”

“I should hope not,” I said. “I carry one myself.”

“I know,” B’russ’r said. “And a beamer. Without both of which, you have said, ‘I feel and am, undressed.’”

Information upload. The Beri seemed fully prepared to write my biography. Or of course my obit, if it turned out that way. At least I’d be assured of accuracy, I reflected–something few obits could claim.

This reflection was, somehow, not a comforting one. “Now–what are the chances of tracing the gun, through the bullets?”

“The two shots at you, hopeless,” he said after half a second. “One on a busy street, long gone. The other cleaned away by Totum and Robbies, several days’ trashloads ago, equally gone. The one in Leake–a great deal will depend on just what that bullet hit on the way in.”

“Let us hope only soft things, sufficient to stop it inside him but not deform it too much.”

One more nod. “Tell me, Knave,” B’russ’r said in what was for him almost a plaintive voice. “Would you have another of those cigarettes? I dislike to be a bother–”

“No bother at all,” I said, and fished out a pack and gave him one, and shook one out for myself.

B’russ’r stuck the thing through his filter and began to chew. Well, Sherlock Holmes had his needle, whatever it was filled with–deadly nightshade, I think. I suppose B’russ’r could have his chomping tobacco. Night had pretty well fallen, and the tower Leake had called VT was a dark thin finger against a darker sky. From Ravenal, and somehow it’s fitting, there isn’t much in the way of constellations, just a scattering of stars, only a few of which have names rather than catalog numbers–all in all, though, about twice the number visible from even a good spot on Earth. A few were out, and the big yellow-orange solo moon as well.

“Do you know,” B’russ’r said, “it would be fascinating if there actually were some connection between all of this and the shootings of my people five years ago.”

Fascinating, I said, might not quite be the word. Myself, I rather liked “impossible”.

“Surely not that,” he said, chewing away.

I tapped ash. "Well–highly improbable," I said, backing off a bit. "What connection could there possibly be? A slug gun–but two slug guns, over a five-year-period, is no great shock."

"Still–" he sighed through a mouthful of Inoson (I suppose) Chewing Pleasure Tube.

"If I could so much as imagine a connection," I began, and then of course I did. "Tell me, B'russ'r," I said. "In what areas of the library did those three Berigot work? I mean, when they were shot, not where they are now."

"Of course," he said. "I will check, and let you know tomorrow morning." He actually chuckled. Berigot don't laugh much–which may of course be a consequence of information upload. "Early tomorrow morning," he added.

"I'll be waiting for it," I said. "Just imagine–all the pieces part of the same puzzle."

B'russ'r chuckled again. "The idea attracts," he said. "It has a certain elegance."

It had more than that for me. It had the promise that perhaps, just perhaps, the Master would not have thought of it first.

Of course, there was always little Robbin. No one knew what Robbin Tress might come up with at any given moment.

But I was after any faint sign of parity with my colleagues. I am not often surrounded by people all of whom are brighter than I am–which may be a statement about the world, and may be a statement about the kind of choices I make. Throughout this job, I kept meeting them.

Such a thing is probably very good for my soul. I hope it is good for something, because it does my ego, in whose care and feeding I am devotedly interested, no damn good at all.

ELEVEN

I SPENT RATHER a difficult night, tossing and turning a good deal. I rang the Master, filled him in on Leake, and laid out the connection with the Berigot shootings of five years before. He took the news of that connection in silence, for the most part—which meant that indeed he hadn't thought of it first. He promised to tell little Robbin as soon as he could call her, which would be the next morning around eleven.

"She is of course upset," he told me. "The meeting did that, and might have been expected to do that. Nevertheless, it may have been good for her. A small taste of normal life."

I took a deep breath, about to say mildly that discussion of a forgery and a theft, with Master Higsbee and a Survivor, was the Hell of a definition of "normal life", but I never got the chance. That rasp of a voice said: "Finished," and the Master hung up.

And after that there was little but tossing and turning. Tossing, that is to say, an interesting salad with an interesting dressing—six or seven varieties of lettuce, thin-sliced radishes, slivered celery and a dusting of grated almonds, in oil and raspberry vinegar—and turning very carefully, three or four times, a small array of loin lamb chops as well, basted in salt, mint and a very little garlic, this deliberately left out of the accompanying salad.

A little more coffee, some of the remaining cheese (notably a variety I'd just found on Ravenal, something the local shop described as "City Four Smoked", which was helpful but nowhere near helpful enough), and I was ready to face an appalling fact: until someone came through with some data (the police, possibly, on the bullet—B'russ'r, on the Berigot who had been shot—anyone else on anything else), I had nothing to do but think.

I have no objection to thinking; after all, it is seldom fatal. But though I know perfectly well that, in most situations, the sensible thing to do is to follow the old, old rule—"Don't just do something—stand there"—I am not temperamentally equipped to do that very gladly. Standing there while you figure out, not just something to do, but the *right* something to do, is almost always correct. But it isn't fun, and it isn't easy.

Here, however, there was one additional difficulty. When I began to think, it dawned on me that I was thinking about something that did not, really, make a very great deal of sense.

Ping had hired me for a very specific job, as he'd said: to find and recover the manuscript of Heinlein's *The Stone Pillow.* But it wasn't Heinlein's manuscript; it was a forgery, though certainly a good one. Why bother to find it and recover it?

If Ping had wanted to leave it to the locals, of course, the question became: Why not? The thing had a value as a curiosity, and finding out how the theft had been managed would be educational for the Library; whatever loophole had allowed the little band of thieves in could then be plugged.

Recovering the manuscript would be educational as well—for the thieves, and for prospective thieves. The fact that Ping could trace and recover a stolen object might just lessen the number of future stolen objects.

More, as Ping himself had said, the thing had been an extremely good forgery. It would certainly be educational for whole groups of people to find out exactly how it had been managed. That might, almost, be reason enough—education of that kind.

But education was all right as an explanation only if it came cheap enough—which I don't. Ping had reached out to hire Gerald Knave, which meant that he had something more serious in mind, and I was damned if I could imagine what.

Nor could I imagine, no matter how I marshaled what facts I had (not enough), why the thing had been stolen at all. It was a forgery, known to be a forgery generally; lots of people were quite familiar with the fact. A good deal of work and time had gone into the theft—that much had been clear since I'd seen the room and talked with B'russ'r for the first time. Who would have bothered—and why?

And it wasn't only the theft. I'd been shot at, twice. Ramsay Leake had been shot at once, with more permanent results. Five years before, three Berigot had been wounded. All this was certainly part of the same picture, wasn't it?

But the picture made no sense whatever.

I contemplated all that for a while, and arrived nowhere at all. So I began to contemplate smaller matters—technical matters.

And when I began to assort those, it struck me that one thing needed a great deal of thinking about. Norman W. Nechs had (by assumption) been a real person, with a real history of sorts, into which the Heinlein forgery could be fitted neatly and without too much strain.

Had he taken a great deal of finding? I mean: Heinlein had certainly been a popular author, selling millions upon millions of his books. A Heinlein fan might almost have been assumed, given the date alone. Not quite—it is a fact, though a sad one, that even in his lifetime there were people who'd never heard of him—but that the man had been a Heinlein fan of some sort was at least a fair guess.

But had Nechs been any sort of special fan, any sort of collector? Had there been a lot of *real* manuscripts, first editions, autographed photos, whatever in that armored hole along with *The Stone Pillow*?

The people who had dug out the hole would of course know. (And had they dug out *The Stone Pillow*? Had they added it themselves? Had it been added just a bit later, when the whole pile was being examined and catalogued—and, if later, with or without their connivance?) But who were these people, where were they, and could they be asked? More, could they be asked by me, or was I going to have to be, to get any answers, some sort of Official Ravenal Grand Central Library Detective?

When it dawned on me who might have the answers to such questions, I found myself smiling broadly. I had not seen the man in some time, and it was going to be a pleasure to make the acquaintance of Charles Hutson Bellemand MacDougal all over again.

Unfortunately, Mac is a morning person. At ten-thirty P. M. (which Mac, who has about four times the normally-sized Scientific Mind, would certainly call twenty-two-thirty, however silly that sounded), I could only shelve the thought for the morrow, and take myself off to bed in at least a cheerful and expectant mood.

I did draft a list of questions first, and leave them next to the phone. I am not in the least a morning person, and when I did call Mac, I told myself, it would be well to have a reminder right there regarding what I was calling him about.

And, for that matter—I am *really* not a morning person—what my name was.

TWELVE

MORNING, GOD DAMN IT.

I got up. I shaved. I dressed. I made faces at myself in the mirror until I could see well enough to count both eyes and only one nose. I made breakfast on the usual automatic pilot, and ate it just as unconsciously, barely knowing what it was. I think, most breakfasts, I could drink instant coffee and never so much as resent it.

And I began, slowly, to think about the telephone. Calls to wait for. Calls to make. I knew perfectly well what sort of delays I was going to run into with Detective-Major Hyman Gross, so I pushed multi on the phone body, set Line A for Receive, and dialed Ravenal Scholarte Locator on Line B.

Locator wanted to give me Mac's public-relations line–any man with two Nobels, even on Ravenal where Nobels do happen, has a public-relations line–but I knew what words to say in what order, and the sweet-voiced mech finally unbelted and told me he was just finishing a class in black-body interactions, and would get my message within a few minutes. I swear I could hear regret in the mechanical voice, unable to be more precise than "a few minutes" because human beings just would not be predictable to the millisecond.

So I said something regretful, and thanked the mech, and hung up, leaving the equipment set for multi. (I always thank mechs, of all sorts. I am not sure what a proper definition of "life" is, but I do feel, whatever the definition finally turns out to be, it is probably better to treat everything as if it were alive, from your Totum to your toothbrush.) And it was actually Mac who phoned first.

"What–in the name of the seven simpering Demons of Maxwell's Magnificent Purgatorio–are you doing on Ravenal, without bothering to tell me about it?"

It's one of those names, as I've said. It's one of those voices, too, a rolling baritone that sounds as if its owner simply gets pleasure out of producing it. "A quick stopover," I said. "Visiting a few people, and not disturbing others. And then something came up."

"Who have you been visiting, who has not been me?" he said. "I have you to thank for two of the most interesting moments of my life so far, and when you actually do manage to find Ravenal–and we must be dull for you, after your usual haunts–you don't even bother to phone me."

I said: "I did bother to phone you, Mac. You're returning it."

"Technicalities," he said. "Not that I want to denigrate the notion of technicalities, Knave, they've been responsible for a Nobel. What's more, one of mine. All the same–well, what is it that's come up, at least? New alien beings? New troubles for Marietta? Who was, by the way, one of those two moments I mentioned a minute or so ago."

I knew that. I knew the other moment, too, and did not regret her quite as much as I regretted Marietta. But Mac was someone with whom you did not compete, not if you were sane–and merely human. "Nothing nearly so exciting," I said, "and the woman involved is Robbin Tress, perhaps not exactly your sort of moment."

A small silence. Mac riffling through the file cards in his mind, of which he has an exceptionally large set. "A fascinating person, from all accounts," he said. "I've never had the chance to meet her, Knave. But what could Robbin Tress have got herself involved in? The woman is almost a recluse–a carefully befriended and surrounded recluse, to be sure, but still–"

"She didn't get herself involved," I said, "I involved her. *The Stone Pillow.*" And there was a little hiss of indrawn breath at the other end.

"I should have known," Mac said. "Forgery, theft–of course, your sort of thing exactly."

"I am not," I said stiffly, "either a thief or a forger."

"Nor am I," Mac said. "In case you were wondering. I was the man who blew the whistle. In fact–" A brief pause. "Oh. That's why you've called."

"Not exactly," I said. "There have been developments. I need to hear exactly how you found out *enough* to blow the whistle."

"Developments?" he said. "Knave, tell all. Where can I meet you? I'll come to your place, whatever luxurious harem it is you're currently inhabiting–"

"In a bit, perhaps," I said. "I know there were differences, when you finally got to doing a complete isotope assay. But why did you decide to do one? The things are complicated, and expensive–"

"Money is no object," he said, and the sentence brought me back to the day I'd met him. He'd said that then, and it hadn't been, and I'd taken on a very odd job on the strength of it–well, on that, and the urging of Marietta Tree, and one thing and another. I found myself briefly regretting Marietta, all over again. There is something about Charles Hutson Bellemand MacDougal that could irritate me greatly, if I didn't like him so much.

And the job had been worth doing for its own very odd sake, anyhow.

"Even so," I said. "You're a careful man–but *that* careful?"

"That careful," he said flatly, and there was a little pause while he realized that I knew perfectly well he was lying through his teeth. He sighed. "Very well, then, Knave, I will come clean for you–but you must promise not to noise this abroad anywhere; I have a reputation to maintain."

"I will be as silent as any one of several gravestones," I said. "Tell me all."

"I have," he said slowly, "low tastes."

I grinned into the phone. "Haven't we all?"

Another sigh. "You don't understand," he said.

I said: "Of course I understand. And while I don't want to pry into your personal enjoyments, I don't really see what they could have to do with isotope assay on a manuscript that–"

"No," he said. "You really don't understand, Knave. The fact is, I read science-fiction. A good deal of it. Privately for the most part–oh, there is a group, a fan club one might say, and we do meet once a month, but for the most part–"

"Wait a minute," I said. "Wait a minute. Is it some deep, dark crime, some sort of manic perversion, to read science-fiction? I do myself, now and again–when it doesn't get too fancily adventurous. I doubt there's anybody working just now to compare with the greats–Heinlein, Sturgeon, Robinson, Haldeman–but a few moderns have written some interesting–"

"It's different for you," Mac said. "Nobody cares what you read–or, unless it becomes necessary for one job or another, if. But there's a spotlight on me, Knave–two Nobels will do that. Even one. Even–well, what you might call a normal Ravenal reputation; in the group, we're all a bit shy of admitting our reading habits. A spotlight has advantages, but it makes trouble as well: if it were generally known that I actually read science-fiction, it would injure me—lower my status, if you like. And I like my status. Silly as it sounds, and silly as it undoubtedly is, I enjoy being looked up to, admired, catered to—being at the top of my particular tree."

I said: "I like it myself, the little I get of it." Then I was quiet for a bit. "You'd think the prejudice would have died out by now," I went on. "It's a harmless pastime, after all."

"It is among the moderns," he said. "Fun and games. Almost none of it is really science-fiction any more. Among the greats—well, the ones you mentioned, and Anderson, and Budrys, and—" He cut himself off with what seemed an effort. I understood; the list could go on for a bit—"among the greats, it was often a means of questioning the way things are. To be exact about it: The Way Things Are." He made the capital letters very audible. "That is never going to be fashionable—or, in my set of intellectuals, acceptable."

He had a point. The ruling intellectual set, throughout most of the Comity, said loudly again and again that they were tolerant of, even glad to hear about, opinions other than their own; and they kept being surprised that there *were* any opinions other than their own. Surprised, and scornful.

"Maybe things were different, back when Heinlein was alive and working," I said.

"I doubt it," Mac said. "What we have—what managed to make it through the Clean Slate War and the troubles after, until someone could find and preserve it—complains often enough of the same sort of attitude. Take *If This Goes On . . .*, for instance. Now there—"

I headed him off. A long chat about the classics would be fun—science-fiction had been one of the highlights of my own scrappy Classical education—but we really didn't have the time for it, and both of us knew it. "You may be right," I said. "But—about the isotope assay—"

He sighed. "Back to business, yes," he said. "Well, I did have a chance to read *The Stone Pillow*. It sounds a great deal like Heinlein. There are some oddities, but even in work we know is his, work that survived in published form, there are oddities now and again, sentences that sound a little off, images that don't come clear—"

"True of any writer," I said. "Even Shakespeare had his off days. Even Chaucer. Even Morgen. Even—"

"Agreed," he said. "Such things didn't make me suspicious. Heinlein was very conscious of style—far more conscious than he appears to be—but even more conscious of substance. He might well let pass a small stylistic discontinuity, might not even realize it was there. But the fact is, Knave, that he never wrote *The Stone Pillow* —never could have."

I blinked. "Why in Hell not?" I said.

"Because he said he didn't—years later. *Concerning Stories Never Written*. You may never have seen it, a short essay meant to be published with the Future History chart." I never had. Mac had clearly read even more science-fiction than I had. "There are arguments that he simply packed the thing away, dissatisfied with it or unwilling to let a story so gloomy actually be published—but the arguments don't ring true to character, to Heinlein's character as we can know it from his work. He'd never have lied about the thing; he'd have avoided mention of it, or told the truth."

I nodded at the phone. "Well, as it turned out," I said, "he *didn't* write it. And that—the essay, I mean—was enough to make for a full isotope assay?"

"I hesitated for a long time. A very long time. But—Knave, this is *Heinlein* we're talking about," he said. "How was I to let some odd scribbler's work go down to the next generation of fans and readers as the work of Robert A. Heinlein?"

I nodded again. "True," I said. "It would never do, not at all."

We gave the thought a little silence. Then I looked at my list of questions.

"I want to know something about the history of the manuscript," I said. "Was it found in the dig itself, at the same time as everything else? And just what was 'everything else'? Or was it perhaps discovered later, by one of the researchers who went back just to make sure they'd gotten the whole load? Was there a lot of other Heinlein material, a lot of other science-fiction material?"

"I wasn't there," he said.

"But you know who was," I said. "You might be able to ask them."

There was about a second and a half of silence, and then he chuckled, a low cheerful sound from a man of low tastes. "We might both ask them," he said. "Come along with me, and we'll find at least one of them—Bitsy will be there for certain, she never misses."

We strive to make our service
As distinctive as our food.
Tell us how we did for a chance to

WIN 1 of 2 $1,000
CASH PRIZES

In the Popeyes Guest Satisfaction Survey Sweepstakes
By calling: 1-800-682-0219
Or by visiting us online at:
WWW.TELLPOPEYES.COM
And complete our online survey for your chance
To win one of these cash prizes and for a chance to

INSTANTLY WIN an iPod®!

- CASH PRIZE -
No purchase necessary. Void where prohibited. Open to valid residents of 50 US States, DC, & Canada (except province of Quebec) 18 and older. Sponsored by AFC Enterprises, Inc.
See www.tellpopeyes.com for complete details.

- IPod® PRIZE -
Sponsored by Empathica Inc.
Must be legal age. Void where prohibited by law.
No purchase necessary. Visit www.tellpopeyes.com for complete details. Apple IPod® prize value of $200 per day.
iPod® is a registered trademark. Apple is neither a participant in or sponsor of this promotion.

POPEYES®

We strive to make our service
As distinctive as our food.
Tell us how we did for a chance to

WIN 1 of 2 $1,000
CASH PRIZES

In the Popeyes Guest Satisfaction Survey Sweepstakes

Welcome To POPEYES

Store # 8581

Sale Number 73161595

DRW 2 Register # 2
*** Here *** Empl # 39
Fri Aug 06, 2010 01:59:22 pm

>	1	2pc COMBO D	7.49
	*	Mild	
	*	Dark	
	*	RG COLESLAW	
	*	BOTTLED WATER	0.20
	*	BISCUIT	

Tax	0.63
Grand Total ================	8.32
Credit Card	8.32

Thanks! For Comments: 1-972-574-6805

Order Number: **257**

I said: "Bitsy? Where? What?"

"At the club meeting," he said. "Tomorrow night, which is convenient—you won't have to wait too long to start getting a few answers. Bitsy Bowyer. She was one of the dig team, and a valued club member."

It was a big moment for one-word questions. "Club?" I said. "Bitsy?"

"The science-fiction club," Mac told me. "The Ravenal Misfits. Bitsy's a member. Do come along, Knave—you might enjoy this."

I might at that, I thought. And someone actually on the dig was going to be a necessary item of my workload, at the very least.

"Where and when?" I asked Mac, and he told me.

THIRTEEN

THE MEETING WAS the next night—which left me with minimal material to think about, unless I did something. I stared into space for a few seconds, drew a deep breath, and began trying to get Detective-Major Gross on the line.

It didn't take nearly as long as I'd been very sure it would; a mention of Ramsay Leake, and a mention of Gerald Knave, seemed to work fairly well as a combination for the usual bureaucratic lock. In about four minutes I had Gross on the line and was asking him about the bullet. Had it come from the same gun that had been tearing up Berigot five years before?

"We can't be wholly sure," he told me.

I shut my eyes for a second. "Weapons ballistics is more or less an exact science," I said.

Gross said, patiently: "It's been five years, man. There may have been other firings from the weapon. There's been some degradation, after all. Any defense lawyer in the city—"

"I'm not asking what a City Two court will accept," I said. "I'm asking what you know."

He grunted. "Oh, it's the same weapon."

"Then there is a connection," I said.

He grunted again. "Unless the gun itself had been passed on," he said. "Three or four times, it might be. It does happen, you know. The person who used it on Leake may not even have known the person who used it five years ago."

It was possible, but: "Most gun owners keep their weapons," I said.

"Most gun owners involved in highly illegal activities—like murder and attempted murder, to give you two—do not."

He had a point, damn it. I admitted it to him.

"We've a weapons registration law in force here," he went on. "Any adult person can buy a gun—but every gun is test-fired, and the records of that firing are filed. We can identify any particular gun as having fired any recognizable bullet."

"And?"

"This one doesn't show up in the records, Knave," he said. "A good many illegal-use weapons don't, after all—there's the usual black market."

Well, there would be. "Another argument against the same shooter being involved," I said sadly. Everything had seemed much simpler ten minutes earlier.

"Right," Gross said. "An illegal gun—and so, very likely to have been passed on quickly. A sensible man would have destroyed the thing five years ago, when he stopped trying to bag Berigot."

"Any other news?" I said.

"Not one single new," Gross said, and hung up.

And the phone rang.

B'russ'r, with news. The Berigot who had been shot, five years before, had all been working, at the time, in the same wing of the library from which *The Stone Pillow* had been so neatly lifted.

That, of course, pinned down the connection—not that there had been any doubt in my mind, but it was something even Detective-Major Hyman Gross would have to swallow—as if the news on the bullet hadn't, all by itself, been wholly persuasive.

Now all I had to figure out was what the connection was. Five years before, the manuscript of the Heinlein probably hadn't been so much as a gleam in an archaeologist's eye; it had only been sitting in the Scholarte for four.

But of course the plan to forge that manuscript might have been a great deal more than a gleam, might have been a full-fledged mote, or even a sizable beam, in somebody's eye. And the first step, obviously, had been to wound (and not kill) three Berigot from the library wing that was going to house the forgery years later.

This did not make the Hell of a lot of sense, when I looked at it calmly. It didn't make any more sense when I threw it down on the floor and screamed at it.

I made some more coffee, an odd variety originally from Queensland, and lit a cigarette, and sat down and thought. And all that day, and all that night, God damn it, nothing of any interest whatever happened, either outside my head or within it.

The next day was, in general, even duller. I poked around the Library trying to find something worth thinking about; I bothered Gross and a number of technicians down at the Police buildings—and I'd have done equally well trying to strike up a conversation with one of my Robbies. Even on Ravenal the things aren't geared for chatter, though many Totums talk well enough, when they're not busy supervising Robbies or doing the heavy work; I finally reached the point at which I could have a small dinner, and went out to find one, being thoroughly sick of my own company.

On Ravenal, as I've said, they make tradition do for imagination a good deal, so I was not entirely surprised to find a nicely expensive place called Blackjack, after a preSpace, equally expensive (for its time) New York City restaurant. I fell in there and ordered Classically: a cheeseburger, fries and a large beer.

The fries brought me back to Heinlein—Fries was Poddie's last name (*Podkayne of Mars*, if you're not keeping up, a short novel that exists in two versions, one Heinlein's and one, in part, his publisher's)—and the cheeseburger, though it was clear that the Blackjack chef was trying hard, didn't quite have the authentic tang of cheap meat. The beer deserves a little paragraph or so to itself, if you don't mind.

The object of alcoholic drinks, Blackjack apparently felt (and it seems to be a common feeling on Ravenal generally, damn it) is to intoxicate the user. Some do this quickly; some, like beer or champagne, do it slowly and, more or less, gently, and there an end of it.

This is wrongheaded. It is function without form. The idea of an alcoholic drink is to assuage thirst and create relaxation at the same time; it is, like most pleasures, a multipurpose gimmick. In order to do this well, the stuff has to taste good.

Most beers don't, though a truly bad beer is not easy to find. A few are worth drinking, and fewer still are worth actually hunting up. The beer provided at Blackjack was none of these things; it was very nearly not there at all.

I drank sixteen ounces of something that reminded me dimly of beer, in a generic sense, provided me with a faint alcoholic glow, and vanished, to reappear later on as waste. I resented the glow; if I'd had no pleasure in the stuff going down, I didn't want some tiny additional pleasure sneaking into me by a back door.

I paid a bill that was not quite as staggering as it might have been in the original Blackjack—I'm reasonably sure that was the name of the old New York City place, though it might have been 21; well, I told myself, I suppose people on Ravenal would know—and went out into the night, found a taxi and gave him the address of the Ravenal Misfits. He actually found the place, which took a bit of doing: it was a warehouse, ancient by Ravenal standards and not very well kept up, with a second floor one-third filled with old crates of something or other—faxprint paper, from the smell—and two-thirds filled with a scattering of chairs, and three long tables. One of the tables had two chairs behind it, and some stacks of paper and books on it, as well as a pile or two of computer disks and other antiquated material. One, off in the left-hand corner as I came in, was filled with ancient magazines in seal, faxprint flyers about events I couldn't quite figure out (TERTIUS WEEKEND 17-20 SEVENMONTH: BYO TOGAE, RON MAGEE CHIEF STIMULATOR, one read), and the third had urns of coffee, setups for tea, and a selection of what seemed to be antique small cakes and cookies. Some of the chairs—arranged in two ragged blocks, about eight by ten chairs to a block—and a lot of the floor space was occupied by a collection of people who looked surprisingly normal; for some reason I'd expected fans of sf to look very odd indeed, and this turned out to be true only of some of them.

FOURTEEN

THE NAME, MAC told me, was highly traditional. Away back before the Clean Slate War, a school or college or university or scholarte whose initials were M. I. T. (for Massachusetts Indefinite Techniques, I think) was the home of an sf club, the Massachusetts Indefinite Techniques Science-Fiction Society, or M. I. T. S. F. S. This was pronounced Misfits for some damn reason, and the Ravenal group was named in its honor. M. I. T. had been, in a very small way, the Ravenal of its time, Mac said, with all sorts of important ideas having been born there—the earliest cyberneticists were M. I. T. people, for instance.

The Misfits, as I was saying, didn't look too misfitted to the actual world. One or two, perhaps—there was a Chandes Washington, for instance, a tall thin fellow with an enormous shock of white hair, a dark-brown complexion, and the wide eyes of someone who had got lost on the way to somewhere forty or fifty years ago, and had never really found his way back to Go. And there was Corri Reges, whose hair was pale blue and who wore small ancient spectacles with wire rims; behind them her eyes glittered very strangely. Corri wasn't fat nearly so much as she was wide; she seemed to be two or three people in extent, all pushed together somehow under one enormous bright-blue jumper.

And there was a medium-height, square-jawed fellow who introduced himself as Max Headroom. I did get the reference—a preSpace show on flat TV, about a character who existed only as a computer construct—but he stood there and explained it to me anyhow, complete with a digest of plot lines from the ancient show, which made no sense to me at all.

Mac did the introducing, for the most part, but there was little formality in the group; I'd walked into a buzz of talk that echoed a bit in the big space, shook some hands when indicated, and found a chair handy to an exit. It seemed the prudent thing to do.

The buzz lessened a bit, but never quite died, when the chairman of the group—they called him President—banged on the central long table with what looked like an antique slide rule.

His name, Mac had told me—he was one of the twenty or so I hadn't shaken hands with yet—was Maxwell Glatz, and he was a short, very hairy type—black coarse hair virtually all over his head and face, with no moustache—in a severe dark-grey jumper that had seen many, many better days. He glared fiercely around at the crowd of people and banged his antique on the table again, and the buzz of conversation slowly died.

"The Sixmonth meeting of the Ravenal Misfits will please come to order," he said. He had a voice that fit his appearance, loud and rasping, an Emergency siren calling for its mate. He waited a few seconds, looking around some more, and then nodded. "Glenda couldn't make it tonight," he said in a more conversational tone; "her stoats are acting up again. She did send over details, if anyone wants to hear the Treasury report."

There was a general groan.

"Dispense with the Treasury report, okay," Glatz said. "Is there any old business?"

"Crain," someone said from the back of the room. I looked around, but which of six or seven men there had made the comment I couldn't tell; it might even have been a deep-voiced woman.

"We are not going to discuss Crain any further," Glatz said firmly. "By the Almighty and All-Powerful Ghu, enough is enough."

"Well," the same voice said, "is he or isn't he?"

This time I caught the speaker, a small, mild-looking fellow in a wool sweater, clenching an unlit pipe that looked to be authentic briar. His expression was a sort of disappointed determination, as if he had been bringing Crain up at every meeting for five or six years.

"He is not," Glatz said. "And he won't be."

Mac—sitting up front, and big enough to block the views of a couple of smaller people behind him—stirred in his chair. "Do you think that's entirely fair?" he said.

"Crain broke the rules," Glatz said. "There are rules, you know."

"Everybody breaks rules, sometimes," Corri Reges said. For a very wide woman she had a surprisingly narrow voice, middle-register viola for tone. "That's no reason to ban him from meetings."

"It all depends on which rule you break, Corri," Glatz said, very mildly, "and why you break it. Crain broke an important rule, and he broke it for no good reason."

"Like calling me Corri," Corri said. "If this is official business, Mr. Glatz, I'm Ms Reges."

Glatz sighed. "That's different," he said. "That's procedure. Crain–well, we all know what Crain did."

"He talked to a reporter," Mac said. "That was a mistake. It doesn't seem to have been fatal."

"Something may appear any day," Glatz said. "In the name of the Great Ghu–any minute."

"I think you're overstating things here," Mac said. "The reporter was a friend of Crain's, he was drunk at the time, he took no notes–"

"Have you ever heard of recording devices?" Glatz put in.

Mac sighed. "He was *drunk* at the time," he said. "Very. To an extreme. From all I have reliably heard, I don't really imagine he could have worked a recording device. He may not have been able to work a pencil. He was not sober."

"Even so," Glatz began, and Mac said:

"The truth of the matter is, you don't like Walt Crain, and you've been looking for a reason to bar him from the Misfits, and you think you've found one."

Corri put in, in a tender little viola-d'amore voice: "And I, for one, am not going to stand for it."

"Nor I," Mac said, and the man at the back of the room said, around his briar:

"Hear, hear."

"I say he's out," Glatz told them all, "and what are you going to do about it?"

Mac rose and looked around him at the rest of the Misfits. "Who," he said, "is ready to hold a new Presidential election?"

Glatz said: "Hey–"

There was a general murmur of Yes and No. To my ear, the Yesses had it, but the margin was not large.

"Or," Mac said into the dying murmurs, "we might just vote on whether to expel Walt Crain."

The Yesses had that one, three to one or better. Mac nodded very curtly at the room, turned back to the Misfit President, and said:

"We could do that, you know. There's precedent."

"In the history of sf fandom," Chandes Washington said—the dark-brown man with all the white hair, in a voice like a sad, lost trombone, "there is precedent for damn near anything."

"True," Mac said. "It's all in Moskowitz somewhere."

(The name was strange to me, but Mac explained it later on; Moskowitz was, I was told, the great historian of early sf fandom, and source of the rule that the main constituent in any sf fan group was a tendency toward faction. "He never actually said that, quite," Mac told me, "but it's written between every lovely, strange line of his histories." Much of Moskowitz, apparently, hasn't survived, but there is enough, according to Mac, to provide a fair notion of the preSpace history, not of sf but of sf fandom. "The dear man lived in a world of his own," Mac said, "and one with only tenuous connections to the rest of the planet at that time—so much the better for fandom.")

"Put the question, then," the man in the back of the room said around his briar.

Somebody called: "Question," and Chandes Washington said, mournfully:

"Hear, hear!"

There was a little silence. Glatz gave an enormous sigh.

"Very well," he said. "The question is: Shall Walton Crain be excluded from all participation in the affairs of the Ravenal Misfits?"

"All official affairs," Corri Reges put in instantly. "However the vote goes, he's going to be welcome at my place."

Small murmurs of agreement.

"All official affairs," Glatz said. "The question is put; show of hands."

Mac made quite a production of turning and counting the hands for exclusion, but he didn't have to; there were a total of five, counting both of Glatz's.

In a defeated little voice, Glatz said: "Those against?" About thirty people raised hands. Some of the Misfits, I noticed, had stayed out of the voting altogether—well, maybe they were guests, like me. Or members of a non-voting faction.

"The motion is not carried," Glatz said.

"And Crain is not barred from the place," Corri Reges said. "Thank God for a little sense, and thank you all, ladies, gentlemen and others."

Glatz sighed. Deeply. "New business?" he said, and Mac stood up again.

"I've brought a guest I'd like to introduce," he said. "He's interested himself in an affair that should be close to all our hearts, and he may want to ask some questions of a few of you. I vouch for him personally–he will be no danger to the club, and will not disclose anyone's membership, or endanger any member."

That sounded just a hair too sweeping, as a guarantee, but I let it pass, looking just as trustworthy and dignified as I felt I could manage.

"If you vouch for him, Dr. MacDougal," Chandes Washington said sadly, "that's good enough for me." There was a general murmur of agreement, and with no further ado whatever Mac turned, motioned for me to stand up, and introduced the members of Ravenal's sf fan club to Gerald Knave.

FIFTEEN

I made it very showy. I walked slowly to the long table, and went around behind it to stand in front of the unused second chair—the Treasurer's chair, I supposed, but Glenda wouldn't be using it, her stoats were acting up again. There had been a little murmur of conversation when Mac gave my name—he hadn't given much else, apparently figuring I'd do my own explaining from scratch, which was nicely helpful—and I looked at the small sea of faces—well, the pond of faces—until the murmur began to die away. Then I said it. I actually did say it.

"I suppose you're wondering why I've called you all here tonight."

They were a dream audience. Laughter, chatter, applause. I think I have had older lines draw better reactions, but not many and not often. I waited for a lull, got a small one, and said:

"I'm here to talk about Robert Anson Heinlein."

Chatter, applause. This time I rode over it. "You all know his work. You all know about *The Stone Pillow.* I'm not sure how many of you know that *The Stone Pillow* is not by Robert Heinlein, but is a forgery concocted by person or persons—"

"Unknown," somebody called out. "We all know that, Mr. Knave." I peered into the pond of faces and found Chandes Washington, still looking lost, but somehow also looking belligerent.

"Knave," I said mildly. "I need to find out a lot about that forgery. How it was planted, how it was dug up, how it was transported here to Ravenal—"

"Ask the police," someone else called. A woman I hadn't met—small, brass-blonde, skin the color of copper and bright, bright blue eyes. She was wearing a tight-fitting, very dark jumper, and she was sitting away over to my right, looking tense.

"I have, I am, and I will," I said. "And I need to ask a lot more than the police. I need to ask some real experts."

"Flattery noted and filed," a smooth little voice said: Corri Reges.

"Most of you are experts on Heinlein, so far as there are any experts," I said. "A few of you may be experts on this particular work—helped to find it or transport it, maybe. Helped to assess it, in one way or another, from reading the thing to doing the final isotope assay."

"That's MacDougal," Washington said unhappily, "and you know him—you must have talked to him already."

A dream audience—and a little more. I thought of a classic remark made, many times, by the preSpace philosopher Will Durant: "*Everybody wantsa get inta de act.*"

"I'll want to talk to more people than Mac," I said. "Individually. I was told that the best way to ask for your help was to come here and do it. So I've done that."

"Why should we?" That was Glatz, at my side but sitting down.

"You're Misfits," I said, turning partway to him for half a second before returning to address the pond. "So am I—in spirit. I've read a little sf myself—" I pronounced it properly, sci-fi—"and I've been reading it since I was a lot younger than anyone here tonight. I won't claim expertise, but—"

"What do you mean by sf?" Corri Reges said. "Today's junk? The sort of thing they adapt for 3V and sell to fools?"

I shrugged. "I mean sf," I said. "Heinlein. Anderson. Niven." A little murmur. I was giving signals, and hoping for "Advance, friend, and be recognized".

"The fast three-week course?" Corri Reges said sweetly.

"I started when I was twelve," I said. "But that's not the important thing."

I was lying about the importance; for this crowd, a history of sf reading *was* the important thing. Without it I was nobody at all. This time I waited for reaction, and got it, from the brass-and-copper blonde. "The thing is forged," she said. "We have no interest in it; why should we have? Why should you have, for that matter?"

"Someone is trading on the reputation of Robert Heinlein," I said. "That gives me an interest. How about you?"

Murmurs. Chatter.

A full minute of it, rising and falling.

Then Max Headroom asked: "But what can we do about it?"

Advance, friend, and be recognized. I relaxed, without moving a visible muscle.

"We can find the forger," I said, "and make the whole thing public."

"But the fact of forgery will be public no matter what we do," the brass-copper blonde said. "That will be enough—and if it isn't, it isn't; putting a name to the forger won't do anything more."

"But it will," I said.. "It'll be a better story—a detective story with a caught criminal at the end of it. The news nets will eat it up. It'll be spread all over—the forgery by itself will only get into library bulletins, a few meetings like this one, and nothing more. Special-interest coverage only."

Mac put in his two cents. "He's right, you know," he said without getting up. "A story like this would be a very big item, for a time."

"But if I'm going to find the forger," I said into the murmurs that followed, "I need a lot of data. From any of you who have it. Some, we can take care of here. More—Mac has my address and phone, and he'll pass it on to any interested parties."

"I don't know," the brass-blonde said. "If it means publicity for us—for the Misfits—well, I wouldn't want people to know I—I was a sf fan, you know. None of us would, Knave. That's why we're careful of outsiders."

Walton Crain and his reporter friend. "I know," I said. "You'll be as anonymous as I can make you—and if you're ever quoted, it will be as experts in your public fields, if that's even remotely possible. I don't mind being known as a fan—"

"For you it's different," Corri Reges said sadly.

"I know it is," I said. "Who cares what I read, as long as I keep moving? But I know it's tougher for you, with reputations to preserve, and I'll do my best to preserve them. Mac can testify that my best has at times been pretty fair."

A small murmur, and a smaller silence. Mac got up, unfolding slowly and spectacularly. "Better than fair," he said carefully. "If there were Nobels for Survivorship, fellow Misfits, Knave's collection would outnumber mine."

At my side, Glatz said: "But—"

That sound was the deciding one; waverers apparently felt they didn't want to be wherever Glatz was. The word fell into dead silence, and then Washington and the brass-copper blonde spoke at once, bass and alto:

"Well, then, let's start work–"

"I suppose it should be all right–"

"All right," I said. "Now, suppose you go on with your meeting, while I take one of you at a time over to a corner somewhere–we'll drink coffee and talk." I didn't wait for approval, because it wouldn't have been approval, it would have been discussion. It is one of my firmest rules: never, unless absolutely unavoidable, ask more than two people to approve of anything at all at the same time. "First, I'd like to talk to a woman named Bitsy Bowyer."

The brass-copper little blonde stood up. "That's me," she said. "Or I, I have never been able to remember which. Shall we go, Knave?"

I gave her a big smile. "Lead on, Ms Bowyer," I said. "I'm right with you."

* * *

I dragged a couple of empty chairs with me, and followed her to the furthest corner of the big place–furthest both from the meeting and from the book-and-magazine table. The refreshment table was between us and the crowd, and much nearer the crowd–we were off in a corner full of old faxprint paper or some such, with enough space to sit and talk. And the first thing she said to me was: "You should know, by the way, that my name isn't Bitsy."

"Sorry," I said. "I thought–"

"Mac must have mentioned me," she said. "I'm Bitsy to old friends. The name is Tabitha Bowyer. And it's not Ms, either."

"Miss?" I said. "Mrs.?"

"Dr.," she said. "Reconstructive archaeology."

"Mac said you were part of the dig team that–"

"That recovered *The Stone Pillow*," she said. "Right, so I was. But we didn't know what we had."

"I'm sure you thought it was genuine–"

She shook her head. "No," she said. "I mean it perfectly literally, Knave: we didn't know what we had. None of us did. We took it out without any really clear idea what it was." She hesitated, and then sighed a little. "Coffee?"

Anything in a good cause, I told myself, and agreed to sample the stuff. She went over to the refreshment table and came back with two coffees–she never asked about milk or sugar; many black-coffee drinkers don't, and whether it's forgetfulness or the assumption that people who drink coffee want to drink nothing but coffee, no additions being possible, I have never quite figured out. She handed me one.

It was even worse than I'd thought it was going to be—weak, tepid, slightly bitter and in a reusable plastic cup. I took two sips, held the cup patiently, and said: "Would you mind terribly explaining that a little?"

SIXTEEN

"IT WAS ALMOST your usual bomb-shelter," she said. "I've been on twelve different reconstructive digs, Knave, and they all look the same–details differ, and after all it's the details that are going to count for us–it's the details we want to dig out–but it was your basic armored hole in the ground, supplied with air, full of detectors that were all fairly useless–knowing whether the ambient temperature is 900F or 250F isn't going to matter to you too much in your armor, after all; what you want to know is, when does it drop below, say, 130F, and a much simpler rig can tell you that–stocked with food containers of some sort, water recycling equipment of some sort, waste disposal–and, of course, the treasures."

"And the corpses."

"Better than half the time," she said, "we don't find the corpses." She took another gulp of her coffee–her fourth or fifth, I thought. The woman was either remarkably tolerant, or had no taste buds at all. "Either whoever owned the hole didn't get to it in time, or left it when things calmed down a bit–some did live through, and leave, you know, though almost all of those were dead within weeks of rejoining the surface–or, to be perfectly frank, God knows what."

I thought about it. "But if they left," I said, "then the hole wouldn't still be waiting to be discovered and dug up, would it? I mean, someone would have found the exit hole, or door, or whatever. Hatch, I suppose."

"Sometimes," she said. "And sometimes the hatch–or exit hole–whatever–has been drifted over since. Sand. Mudslides. Earthquakes. There were quite a lot of earthquakes for the first fifty to seventy years after the War."

"I can see how there might have been," I said. "But in this case there was a corpse."

"There was indeed," she said, and took in more coffee. Amazing woman. "Norman W. Nechs. Dentist, I think. Possibly State Patrolman, possibly some sort of honorary police semi-official. Fan of sf. Collector. And jackdaw."

I blinked. "Jackdaw?"

"Trade term," she said. "People who store things they can't use. What Norman W. Nechs had done was take what he undoubtedly considered to be his most valuable possessions, seal them in a drum full of nitrogen and a little argon under slight pressure—not a bad combination for preservation of manuscript—make the drum vacuum-tight—and just store it away."

"I suppose he thought that, when he came out—"

"He didn't think," she said flatly. "He didn't store anything to open that drum with safely. And he couldn't have assumed he'd come out into a world that would provide him the technical facilities to do the job."

I thought about it for a minute. A nice heavy drum, tough to break into, sealed vacuum-tight, contents under slight pressure—no, not the sort of thing you'd crawl out of your armored hole and pop open with your thumb. "No tools for opening it?" I said. "None at all?"

She shrugged. "I suppose, given a small home workshop of some sort—which we didn't find—and a few days, he could have rigged something that would open the drum without either blasting the contents to shreds or blasting Norman W. Nechs into a puddle. But there was nothing ready in the shelter to do the job; he hadn't thought it out that far. Many didn't."

"So you opened it—" I began, and she said:

"The Hell we did, Knave. We had a fair idea what was inside—manuscript, paper of some sort, some metal object—but not any more than that; it takes better spy rays than we've got to get fine detail. What we knew was that the person who'd made that shelter, who'd put this stuff in a sealed drum inside an armored hole, thought it had great value. That didn't mean he'd been right—people value the damnedest things, even today, and people were no different back before the Clean Slate War—but we had to act as if he had been. We almost decided at once not to open the drum on Earth at all—we discussed loading it on board and opening it when we got back here. But that seemed a bit much—and expensive; we'd have to ship the drum itself and the inside atmosphere as well as the contents, and all we were interested in were the contents. The drum wasn't much of an artifact, and there seems to be quite enough nitrogen and argon around already."

A long speech, and it required more coffee; she got up, refilled her cup, and took a swig before sitting down again. Amazing.

"By the way," she said. "I'm sorry to have been stiff with you—by all means call me Bitsy."

"Fine, Bitsy," I said. "Call me Knave." She looked at me, just the least little bit suspiciously. "Everyone does," I said. "Honestly."

She shrugged. "Very well," she said. "When we—"

"One moment," I said. "You'll pardon me for asking, but just who are the 'we' here? The dig crew, I mean. And are any of the others Misfits?"

Swallow of coffee. "Do you mind if I smoke, Knave?" she said.

The terrible stuff was actually relaxing her. "Not at all," I said. "I'll join you, in fact." I looked around, saw a couple of ashtrays shining on the refreshments table, and rescued one. I put it on my knee, fished in a pocket and came out with an Inoson tube. Bitsy's eyebrows went up; well, most cigarettes *aren't* wrapped in red.

She dug out some of her own—I recognized a local blend, a little mild for my taste and wrapped in dull grey—and a small black holder with some sort of cut-glass jewelry at its far end. She stuck her cigarette in the holder, stuck the holder between her teeth, and I lit us both up.

"Only five of us at the dig by then," she said. "We'd had more at the start, but once we broke in, and got down to the detail work, more than half the team went on to another dig. The doormen, we call that part of the crew—we need them to crack the door open, and that's the extent of it. A much smaller crew takes care of matters from there on."

"Five of you, then," I said.

She nodded. "One of them is a Misfit—Dean Rell. He's here tonight—you might want to talk to him next. The others—well, Freda Hocksher, a very good woman on electronic antiquities—Gro Rouse—that's Grosvenor, you may have heard of him, rather old for actual dig work, but he's always loved it—and Paula Shore, who's quite a comer. Only Dean is a Misfit—the others know nothing whatever about sf, and Grosvenor, for one, would be absolutely shocked to find that Dean and I actually read the low stuff. Do you want pencil and paper, Knave?"

I'd made my notes where I usually make them, in my skull. I find it handier that way, most of the time. "Thanks, I'll be all right. So you opened the thing right there?"

"Well," she said, "not right there at the dig, Knave—we wanted the safest surroundings we could get, right from the start of things. And those are in what used to be southeastern Oregon—interesting coincidence, isn't it?"

"Fascinating," I said. "I suppose it *is* a coincidence?" But I couldn't see how it could have been anything else; if the forged Heinlein had been set in Oregon because the treasure was going to get itself unwrapped in Oregon, I couldn't come close to imagining a chain that would make that "because" even remotely sensible.

True, very little about any of this made sense; somebody had very carefully stolen something which had almost no real value, and had missed me twice, hit three Berigot (five years before) and killed Ramsay Leake dead, all as part of the same damn package. But Oregon was a bit too much; that had to be a coincidence, I was sure. So, within reason, was she.

"I should think so," Bitsy said. She tapped ash into the tray on my knee. I did the same. "There are university facilities there—the Western buildings of NA Collegium, and closest to the dig."

"So you opened the thing at NA Collegium West," I said, "and the Heinlein was inside."

Bitsy looked at me very carefully. "In fact, we didn't," she said. "I'm trying to give you every detail, Knave. We thought about it—we even began plans with the people at NA Collegium. And then we decided—why not be entirely safe? Why not come back to Ravenal, and open the thing here?"

"You brought the unopened drum back from Earth to Ravenal?" I said. She nodded. "Despite the expense." She nodded again. "And you're sure it was unopened—from the dig until wherever the Hell it was you finally cracked the thing."

"Perfectly sure," she said. "It was in Cargo, no way to get to it en route. And nobody opened the thing on Earth—no equipment for it nearer than Oregon, which is some distance from Uta, where the dig was."

I thought for a minute. Perhaps, just perhaps, someone had figured out a way to break into Cargo space on a ship traveling through space-four. All that would take would be a brand-new theory for space-four.

Anything else seemed probable by comparison.

"And when the pie was opened?" I said.

She blinked. "Pie? The drum, you mean? Well, Knave, I wasn't there. It's as special a job as—as bomb disposal, you see. We waited—the dig crew—three floors away from the shop where they opened it."

"So you don't know for certain that the Heinlein had been in the drum before it was opened here," I said.

"Not for–not for absolutely certain, no," Bitsy said. "But we assumed–"

"Naturally," I said. "And what else was in the damn drum?"

Bitsy smiled. "Only a science-fiction fan would remember in any detail, four years later," she said. "A signed copy of Heinlein's *The Menace from Earth* in what was called a paperbacked edition–a real rarity. Two other signed books–*Oath of Fealty* by Niven and Pournelle, of which six other copies are known to exist, and Poul Anderson's *The Earth Book of Stormgate*, not really a rarity today, but we don't have many signed copies, and this one is in fine condition. A paper certifying that Norman W. Nechs was in fact a professional dentist–he may have had some sort of police job as a public service, we can't be wholly sure–a diploma, whatever they were called, that identified him as D. D. S., official dentist. Some other published books, I can't recall just which. And a metal plaque, commending him as most congenial dentist at a convention or gathering of some sort in Taos, New Mexico." She grinned. "I told you he was crazy."

SEVENTEEN

"SO YOU TOSSED the diploma and the plaque–"

"The diploma and the plaque are in the Scholarte museum," she said a little stiffly. "Artifacts. They have value–if not precisely the sort of value Norman W. Nechs thought they had, whatever the Hell that was."

"And the rest–"

"The two books went for testing at once, of course. So did the Heinlein manuscript. Those tests were passed, easily."

Another second or so of thought. "And has anyone tested the two books since finding out the manuscript was forged? Or the plaque and the diploma, for that matter?"

Bitsy nodded. "Of course," she said. "That began instantly. Recreating a bound book, well enough to pass all other tests, is a formidable challenge to anyone–I couldn't do it myself, even ignoring the isotope question. But we were obviously faced with great technical facility; anything seemed possible. Anything still does; testing on the books is not yet complete. It's very slow work; we want as little damage to the books themselves as possible, of course."

"Naturally," I said. "How soon after the pie–after the drum was opened did you see the manuscript?"

Bitsy thought back. "Perhaps an hour," she said. "I wasn't the first to see it, Gro was. He was very anxious about the drum; he did feel it might contain something of importance. I think the bit of metal fascinated him most, but that's only my guess. By the time they'd got the thing open, he was standing outside in the hall."

I nodded. "But within an hour–"

"More or less," she said. "I wasn't clocking it, you know."

"–more or less," I said, "you did see the manuscript?"

She nodded. "Seems impossible, doesn't it?"

"Not quite," I said. "I'm going to have to talk to some other people."

"Gro, you mean," she said.

"Well, him too," I said. "But mainly, whoever actually opened the damn thing. That's the point: when was the forgery slipped in? Before or after opening the drum?"

"If it was before opening the drum," she said, "it might have been a forgery away back before the Clean Slate War; Nechs may have bought it thinking it was genuine. The man was a fool in any case, and—"

I was shaking my head. "It won't work that way," I said. "If the forgery were as old as everything else in the drum, all the isotopes would have checked out nicely." I sighed. "No, someone put the thing in—either at the dig, or here on Ravenal."

Bitsy crushed out her second cigarette. "You mean it's one of us," she said. I shook my head again.

"Not necessarily," I told her.

"But probably."

"Probably," I said. "You said Dean Rell was also a sf fan?"

"Of course he is," she said. "He's here But Dean wouldn't—well, you'll meet him. You can't believe—" She paused. "The fact is, I'm the one who can't believe it—not of any of us. Dean, Gro, Paula, Freda Hocksher—you might as well believe I did it."

"Well—" I said. Bitsy nodded.

"Of course you might," she said. "Why not? I'm as likely as anybody else, as far as you know. But I didn't do it. And I can't believe any of the others did, either."

"It would take someone very familiar with Heinlein's work to do a decent job," I said. "That points to a fan."

"A Misfit, probably," she said. "Fans tend to stick together, to cluster—not only because it's rather a low taste, or so people think, but because we like to talk about our interests. People do, you know." She hesitated just a hair. "But I simply can't believe that one of us did such a thing. You don't know these people, but I do. Dean wouldn't harm a fly. Not a fly. Not the whisker on the head of a fly."

"And the others?"

"Freda Hocksher is a dedicated worker," she said. "A plugger, and a dependable person on any dig. I've worked with her before—we opened a hole in New Mexico together six years ago. Some fine artifacts, silver coins, ancient slug guns. There'd been water seepage there—it does happen, the water table's shifted quite a lot since the holes were dug—but two of the slug guns were in good enough shape for real restoration; they're working models, now. In the museum, of course."

"Paula Shore, Grosvenor Rouse," I said.

"Paula's a youngster—bright, quick, ready for anything. Honest as the day is long, Knave. And Gro—the idea is ridiculous. He's got standing in the field, very great standing. Besides, he doesn't know anything about sf, and cares less. He'd be lost, faced with the job of trying to construct a believable Heinlein manuscript."

"And the other Misfits?" I said. She shook her head. Violently. "Not even Glatz, say? Or Chandes Washington, Corri Reges, Max Headroom—"

"Why those?"

"No special reason," I said. "They look a little odd, somehow—no offense. They may be a lot odd."

"So may anyone," Bitsy said icily. "You might be a bit odd yourself, Knave."

I shrugged. "Hell, I *am* a bit odd," I said. "Everybody is, more or less. But I know I didn't forge the manuscript, or plant it with the rest of the things—or steal it, for that matter."

She scowled at me. "Well, I know *I* didn't," she said. "And the others—"

"I'll try to find out what they know," I said.

"They didn't do it," Bitsy said. "This is Heinlein, after all. They'd have too much respect. Any fan would."

I sighed. "So a fan couldn't have done it," I said. "Too much respect. And someone who wasn't a fan couldn't have done it—not enough background. And that leaves nobody at all."

She sighed too. "I know," she said. "Somebody did it. I just can't imagine who."

Just at that moment, neither could I.

EIGHTEEN

DEAN RELL WAS an entirely different kettle of fish, if you'll pardon the Classical allusion. He turned out to be a tiny man with a red-brown crew-cut, very heavily corrective contact lenses tinted a bright green, and a jumper that fit as tightly as an antique corset. Bitsy Bowyer had gone and fetched him, and then herself retired back to the meeting, and when he sat down he asked me if I'd mind not smoking, tobacco smoke irritated his throat.

About three in ten of the Misfits were smoking at any given moment, but of course I was sitting very close to him. I stubbed out my current Smoking Pleasure Tube, ported the ashtray back to its table and returned with a cheery smile. "Thank you, I'm most grateful," he said in a clear, high voice a bit like B'russ'r's. "What would you like to know?"

"You were on the dig with Dr. Bowyer," I said.

"There were eleven of us," he said. "I was among them, yes."

I nodded. "Five in the dig crew. You found the drum –"

"We found, actually, a great deal," Rell said. "A mass of survival equipment, of course–lighting and wiring, a waste-disposal and recycler arrangement, hundreds of cans of food–quite the usual thing, as far as that went. Nothing we haven't seen a good many times before, all according to the books. Very little originality among these people, you know; everything had become a sort of ritual."

"Well, there are only so many good ways to arrange–" I began.

"I suppose so," Rell said wearily. Some distance from us, the meeting was going on. Voices had become raised; Corri Reges was objecting to something, and it was a little surprising how well that small voice carried. I couldn't quite distinguish the words, and didn't try. "But the sameness of the digs does get to one after a bit," Rell said.

"Beyond the survival equipment–" I said.

"Books," he said. "Many in remarkably good condition–the dryness of the air had been a great help, though of course there was deterioration. Photographs—most of them of people we can't identify, or places we can't really locate precisely now, but valuable despite that, of course, as showing details of the daily life of the time and approximate place. Recordings; this one was a collector of jazz, and had forty or fifty cassette-tapes of jazz musicians from about 1920 to about 1945. Or was that—no, I think the jazz recordings were from that dig."

I stopped him for a minute while he explained what a cassette-tape was, but we needn't bother with it here; it's archaic, and I haven't yet found any use for the knowledge. "And the Heinlein," I said.

"In its special drum," Rell said. "Yes. Of course, we didn't know what it was until we got back here and had it opened, but we were quite excited about it; if the man thought those things valuable enough for very special protection, there was at least the chance that he'd been right."

"That's what Dr. Bowyer said," I put in. "But you weren't right there when the drum was opened, were you?"

"We were as close as we could get," he said. "I think Bitsy—Dr. Bowyer—was the first into the room, but we were all very close behind."

I nodded. "I understood that Dr. Rouse was—"

"Oh, Gro," Rell said. "Gro was waiting outside the door—literally outside the door. But I think, even so, Bitsy beat him in at the announcement. I can't be sure after all this time, you know."

"And the Heinlein did come from that drum?"

"Where else could it have come from?" he said. "We didn't have the thing in our pockets."

* * *

I SPOKE TO a few others at the Misfits meeting. Only Corri Reges seemed helpful at the time.

"I think it's terrible," she said. "Somebody trying to imitate Heinlein, of all people."

"Well," I said, "a lost Heinlein manuscript would certainly be very valuable."

"Oh—valuable," she said, and snorted. As snorts go, it was a fairly charming sound, believe it or not. "It isn't the money, Knave. It's the idea that somebody tried to pass himself off as Robert Heinlein. It's like trying to pass yourself off as—I don't know, Shakespeare. Charlemagne. Fermi."

"Who would do such a thing?" I said.

"Somebody with a warped view of the world," Corri Reges said. "Somebody with no respect for greatness. He must have been crazy to think he could get away with it, whoever did it."

"But he almost did get away with it," I pointed out. "If the isotope assay had checked out right down the line, no one would know *The Stone Pillow* had been forged."

Corri snorted again. "Not so," she said. "Not so at all, Knave. Many of us had our suspicions. I know MacDougal thought something was wrong with the manuscript right from the beginning."

So Mac had said. "Were you suspicious?" I said, knowing the answer I'd get; whatever she'd actually thought at the time, by now Corri was certain to believe she'd been suspicious from the moment she first heard of the thing.

"Lots of us were suspicious," she said. "Max Headroom was sure something was wrong. So was I. So was MacDougal. So was Walton Crain."

Perhaps she was reading her current views back into her past. But I thought she might be telling me accurately about others–she'd have no particular motive to add them to the list of suspicious bystanders. Quite the reverse, in fact; it always feels better to have been the one person alone who detected the truth.

"Why did you all think something was wrong?" I said.

"Well, it had to be," she said. "Heinlein *said* he didn't write the story. He wouldn't have lied about it, not Heinlein. And it just didn't sound like him. Not when you looked close, and if you knew a lot about his work."

Mac had pointed out that Heinlein had stated he'd never written the story. But he'd also said the thing sounded a lot like Heinlein.

Maybe Corri Reges knew more about Heinlein's work than Mac did. Corri, and Max Headroom, and Walton Crain.

I talked to Chandes Washington a little later, and he told me he'd suspected from the start, too. But he had thought the work sounded "very Heinleinesque, very much like the Heinlein of, say, 'The Roads Must Roll.'"

"The style alone was convincing," I said.

"Oh, very convincing," he said. "Whoever did this knew an awful lot about the author's work. This couldn't have been done by someone who'd just read a couple of pages of something."

Which brought me back to the puzzle Bitsy Bowyer had tossed me a small while before—a Heinlein expert couldn't have done it (too much respect for the work), and no one else could have (not enough background). It was one more small impossibility to add to all the others: the theft that made no sense, the valuable forgery that was almost entirely valueless—the traceless entry into the room, and the traces all over the case the manuscript had been taken from.

I got addresses for everyone I'd spoken to, and a few—like Walton Crain—I hadn't yet met. By the time the meeting broke up and I was back in my apartment, it was too late to pick up the phone, but I knew perfectly well how I was going to start the day, after I'd had some sleep, and I did.

NINETEEN

THE MASTER WAS more than fascinated. "You have found a few extremely lovely patterns," he told me in that rasp of a voice.

"Glad you're pleased," I said. "All they say to me is that they make no sense."

There was a faint suggestion of dry chuckling at the other end of the phone. "It is the perfection of the nonsense, of course, that fascinates," he said.

"Somebody stole a manuscript known to be a forgery," I said. "Why? Ping is willing to go to great lengths–me–to get it back, though since it is a forgery it has no great value. Why? Whoever stole the thing passed into the room it was kept in like a ghost–and then left obvious traces all over the manuscript case. Why?"

"You see, Gerald?" the Master said cheerfully–or as cheerfully as that voice, and that personality, could manage to sound. "Nonsense, and quite perfect."

"A Heinlein expert couldn't have done the forgery–he'd have too much respect for Heinlein. But nobody else could have done it–not enough background for the job. And the damned thing was sealed in a drum, at the bottom of a Survivalist's hole, for nearly three hundred years, and was forged about four years ago. Possibly five."

"There are explanations for all of these things," he said. I sighed.

"Tell me some."

"For the sealed drum," he said, "of course there is the obvious: someone put the forgery into the stack, so to speak, after the drum was unsealed."

I sighed again. "You've heard what Rell and Bowyer told me," I said. "There wasn't the Hell of a lot of time for it."

"Gerald," he said patiently, "it need not have taken very much time. After all, we do not know whether the technicians who opened the drum actually looked inside it, or knew what they saw if they did. Until members of the–ah–dig crew arrived, the drum may well have been open, but unrifled, so to speak."

"And one of the dig crew brought the manuscript in, in his pocket?"

"Or under his jumper, or in her handbag," he said. "Or none of them brought it in, and it was there all along."

I blinked. "But it couldn't have been in the drum–"

"No," he said. "But in the room, perhaps. For one of the technicians to place inside the drum as soon as it was opened. I doubt they watch each other with any great effectiveness; there would not be a need for that degree of care, and human beings are normally lazy and careless."

"Possible," I said. "Even obvious."

"There is, however, one additional question," the rasping voice said. "Consideration might lead to some result."

I took a deep breath, fished for a cigarette and remembered in time not to light one while on the phone with Master Higsbee. "Go ahead," I said.

"The manuscript was found in a drum, in the Survivalist-hole of a person who was a fan of science-fiction–I myself am not, it seems a vain pursuit–and a collector. He owned and saved other signed volumes, you said."

I shut my eyes. I saw very clearly what was coming, and it had not occurred to me before. "Oh, God," I said.

"Precisely," Master Higsbee said. "How could anyone have known that Norman W. Nechs read and even collected science-fiction, and kept some valuable science-fictional items in a sealed drum? But the manuscript was right there to be placed with the drum contents."

I said it again: "Oh, God." And I added: "Nobody could have known. Nobody could know what was in the damned hole until somebody dug it out. Unless they were all in on it all eleven of them, it hadn't been dug out before they got there–they'd have noticed traces."

"And?"

I gave him the rest of it. "There's no way for news of the dig to get to Ravenal before the dig crew got there. The dig crew *was* the news. Space-four transmission might have given somebody on Ravenal a sketch of the dig beforehand–say a few hours, possibly as much as a day beforehand–but there are two things wrong with that."

"Yes?" he said.

"First, nobody had such a transmitter—they're not all that common."

"I know they are not," the Master said. "You yourself own one, and have some pride—justifiable, I am sure—in its rarity and value."

"Sure," I said tiredly. It was early in the morning—well, ten o'clock, which is early for me when I can so arrange things—and I was already tired. "Nobody there would have had one. Not a chance in a million. And second—providing a day's lead time, and it probably wouldn't have been that much, doesn't do any good: it must have taken months to get that forgery ready."

"I should say perhaps a year," the rasping voice said.

"So what good would a day's lead time have been?"

"You put it very clearly," he said. I swear he sounded amused. Distantly amused, but amused.

"It's another impossibility," I said.

"Charming," he told me. "I am more than fascinated. The pattern you have showed me is very lovely, Gerald."

"I'm glad you're pleased," I said with pardonable bitterness. Master Higsbee gave that distant chuckle again.

"You should be," he said.

* * *

AFTER A VERY little more conversation, I got around to my request. If I'd been talking to virtually anybody else, I'd have made it an order; I'd hired him on, so to speak, days before. But one does not give orders to the Master.

"I will speak to the dig crew members you have questioned," he said, "as well as the few others—Washington, Crain, Reges—you wish added. After having done so, I will consult with Robbin, ask what questions of her I can find in my skull, and report back to you."

"Meanwhile," I said, "I'll be doing some questioning of my own."

"I am sure you will, Gerald,:" he said. "And do try, in the interstices between questions, to do a little thinking as well. Finished."

Right. Finished.

TWENTY

ABOUT NINETY SECONDS after I put the phone down, it rang again, and when I picked it up more bad news rose up to bite me. I said: "Gerald Knave," and a voice I recognized said:

"I am calling, first of all, to query you about progress."

Ping Boom.

I didn't have much in the way of a progress report. I'd decided the moment I got the news not to tell Ping that the death of Ramsay Leake was connected to his theft—and hoped I could keep him from finding out that the wounded Berigot were a part of it too.

Why? you may ask. I wanted Ping as calm as possible at all times. It is always a good idea to keep the person who's hired you very calm and peaceful; if he gets nervous, he will be calling you or dropping by to visit you every fifteen seconds, telling you, and maybe believing, that he's trying to check on your progress, and possibly help out a bit here and there—but really looking for very little more than reassurance. He's hired a professional, and one of the largest duties of any professional is the duty of sounding professional—of sounding reassuring.

It's a damn bore at the best of times, and an unbelievable disturbance at the worst, and nothing more cheerful anywhere in between. It's a duty I avoid every chance I get.

"I'm collecting facts," I said, as briskly and professionally as I knew how. "I think you'll understand that it takes some time—"

"Have you made any actual progress?"

I didn't hesitate for a second. "A pattern is beginning to come clear," I said. "But there's really nothing to talk about so far, and—"

"It's been several days," he said.

"This was a very unusual sort of theft," I told him, something he already knew. The police, after all, had had the thing all to themselves for a couple of days, and hadn't arrived anywhere in particular. "I've been consulting with a variety of people, and—"

Like Dean Rell, he was one of those people who had spells of not allowing you to finish a sentence. "We need that manuscript," he said. "And we need it quickly."

Well, every bit of bad news has a silver lining. It was a chance, just maybe, to clear up one small bit of the puzzle. I said: "Why?"

There was a small, strangled pause at the other end. Then Ping said: "What?"

"I asked why you need it in such a hurry," I said. "For that matter, why you need it at all. The thing is a forgery. It'll be filed away somewhere, once you have it again, and nobody will ever go to see it."

Ping said, in the coldest voice I'd yet heard from him: "That is none of your business."

"I need all the facts I can get," I said. "I usually do. It's part of the job. That's how I get things done."

"The only fact you need is that we require that manuscript," he said in the same voice. "You have been hired—at an exorbitant rate, I might add—to recover it."

I took a breath. "I need to know what it is I'm looking for," I said. "If the thing is actually a forgery—"

"There's no doubt of that," Ping said.

"—then what do you need it for? And why the hurry?"

"The hurry," he said, as patiently as if he were explaining matters to a small child, "is simply that we want the job done. Done. Completed. Over with."

"But why do you want the job done? This isn't idle curiosity—"

"Knave," he said, "my refusal to reply isn't idle, either. When do you think you'll be able to lay hands on the thing?"

"As soon as I can," I said. "I can't put a time on it—things don't work like that. I'll report in the second I have news for you."

"You do that," he said. "You be very sure and do that."

I sighed. "Look here," I said mildly. "I'm at work. This is what I do. I'm trying to do your job for you. When it's done, you'll know about it, because I'll tell you. Until it's done, I may not have any news at all."

"That's an incredibly arrogant—"

"That's the way I work," I said, just as mildly. "Sometimes I get results. I get them better, and faster, when I'm given all the facts—and I get them better and faster when I am left the Hell alone to go and get them."

"I've told you everything I could," Ping said. "Days have passed. As far as I can see, nothing much has happened. Knave—"

Another sigh. It has occurred to me now and then that all the people who hire me are really the same person. "If you could see far enough," I said, a bit less mildly, "you wouldn't have had to hire me. You have hired me; I'm not doing anything except your job here. I'd take it very kindly if you'd let me do it."

There was one exactly right thing to do—bark: "Finished," and hang up—but you'd have to be Master Higsbee, I decided, to bring it off. I stayed on the phone and listened to him try not to sputter for a couple of seconds.

Then he said: "I'll expect regular reports from you."

"I'll report whenever I have anything to report," I said. "I'm busy now—sorry. 'Bye."

I actually waited for Ping to say goodbye before I hung up. I have no idea why.

A few minutes later, I discovered I actually did have something to do, and I was in a fine, irritable state to go and do it.

I could go over to police headquarters and bother Detective-Major Hyman Gross.

TWENTY-ONE

POLICE HEADQUARTERS WAS a rather small square building with two green globes at either side of a big entrance–a real door, not a holo. Once again, Ravenal was opting for tradition as a substitute for almost anything else, this time a tradition that went back to preSpace motion pictures–2D, most of them. I'm not sure whether real police-stations, in any country in the preSpace world, ever looked like the one I saw on Ravenal, and possibly I ought to check with a reconstructive archaeologist or two, but it seems unlikely on the face of it: the place looked as if it had been built out of old Earth sandstone, or possibly cheap concrete, all of it a dull and dingy grey, with medium-sized glassex windows that had authentic-looking bars on them for some damn reason. To keep the police in? To keep citizens out? They were absolutely useless, since the glassex was, as usual, both unbreakable and permanently sealed in.

And the green globes, on high stands or low pillars–about seven feet off the ground–didn't seem very decorative and served no purpose I could understand. They did tell you the place was some sort of police-station (if you had a background in preSpace motion pictures, where a lot of such buildings did seem to turn up), but a sign saying Police Station would have done the same job, been less of a bother altogether, and required nothing of the inquiring passerby but simple literacy.

There were four stone steps between the globes, leading up to the door. I climbed the damn steps, cursing tradition under my breath, pushed open the door, and went inside. The interior was Ravenal's other face; when they're not being traditional, of course, they're being state-of-the-art, and then some.

Everything that wasn't either people or computers was glassex: desks, chairs, railings, dividers. The walls were, like the outside of the place, something that looked like sandstone, but they were the only opaque objects in that big entrance hall, except for the signs. The signs were thin metal, all painted a restful green and bearing directions in deep red. This sounds as if they were easier to read than in fact they were; it took a little blinking to get the red into focus against the background.

Inquiries, Forensics, Records, and a few others . . . and over to my right a sign with an arrow that said *Detective Squad.* If Gross was going to be in his office, he'd be at the end of whatever path the arrow was indicating, and I followed it a few yards to a flight of sandstone stairs with a glassex railing. Cursing tradition some more, I went up the stairs to a second-floor hallway. The hallway had some closed doors along it on both sides—real doors again, and this time made out of what looked to me like real wood, though I'm no expert—and most of the doors had nothing on them but numbers.

The one at the end of the hallway on the left said *Detective Inquiries,* which was, after all, what I was planning to do, make some Inquiries of a Detective. I knocked on it, and a voice I didn't know said loudly: "About time, come on in."

I found a knob, turned it, and the door opened. As I got the door open, the same voice said:

"Put it down on Terry's desk. Thanks."

"Don't mention it," I said. "Put what down?"

"Coffee," the voice said. "The coffee, what did you think I meant? Just—oh. Who the Hell are *you*?"

The room had three large desks in it, side by side from near the door to away over at the right. There was a computer screen on each desk, and all three desks were littered with faxprint papers of all sizes, shapes and even colors—white, blue, pink. The desks looked like wood, too, and so did the chairs that went with them. The only person in the room was a medium-sized fat man sitting behind the desk furthest to my right, out of sight until I'd come some steps into the room. He seemed absolutely hairless, and he was wearing a slightly soiled white shirt with an open collar. He also wore a pair of rimless spectacles, which he pushed back along a wide snub nose.

"I'm looking for Detective-Major Gross," I said. He nodded.

"Why?"

"Because I need to talk to him," I said.

"He'll be back in a minute," the fat man said. "What do you need to talk to him about? And who are you—start with that, all right?"

He seemed almost friendly, for a police official. "Gerald Knave," I said. "I'd like to ask him some questions about—"

"Jesus H. Christ," the fat man said. "You're Knave? Hyman curses you out almost the same as if you were a citizen. He usually goes a lot lighter on strangers and tourists."

And I hadn't really started to bother the man yet. "What has he got against me?" I said.

The fat man shrugged, a miniature mountainous gesture. "No idea," he said. "He thinks you're a pest. Maybe you are a pest. I'm Dunc Yeager, by the way—Detective-Lieutenant."

I went across to his desk and stuck out my hand. "Nice to meet you," I said. "I'm not any more of a pest than I absolutely have to be. I hate pests."

"Always nice to hear," Yeager said, "assuming it's true. Which I do not. You're from where, now?"

"Out of the everywhere," I said, "into the here. As far as it goes, I'm from here—officially. I've been hired by the Library."

"The what?"

I sighed. "First Files Building," I said. "Ping Boom, Manuscript Division."

Yeager nodded. In a very patient voice, he said: "Hired to do what? If you don't mind, of course."

"Hired to recover something," I said. "A manuscript that seems to have been misplaced."

"And that takes you up here to talk to the Detective Division?" Yeager said. "Hyman is mostly homicide—so am I, for that matter. Not that we don't get involved in other things, as needed—or as the mood takes us. Out of the everywhere—very pretty."

"A preSpace poet," I said, and tried to remember which one. Tennyson? Eliot? Chaucer? "Pay no attention to it," I said at last, giving up the search as a bad job. Perhaps Bitsy Bowyer would know. Or some other archaeologist. Or of course Master Higsbee. "I think Detective-Major Gross is working on a case that connects with my job."

Yeager had no eyebrows to speak of, but his forehead wrinkled as if he were trying to raise them. "You know what he's working on?"

"Ramsay Leake," I said. "I saw him at the scene. Talked to him there."

"And since," Yeager said. "I remember. I said—he curses you out a good deal. Now you want to—"

The door slammed open and I turned around to see Gross coming in. His eyes looked just as big and protruding as ever. He slammed the door behind him, blew out his breath, and said: "You."

"I," I said. "I've got some questions."

Gross snorted. "I have no answers for you," he said. "I am not going to have any answers for you. I've work to do, Knave, and if you don't mind—"

"But I do," I said mildly. "I'm not just some gink off the streets. I need some answers, and the Library needs—the First Files Building needs some answers, and B'russ'r B'dige needs some answers—"

"Oh, God," Gross said. He sat down behind the desk next to Yeager's with an enormous sigh. "As if I had nothing else in this dark world to do. Look, now, Knave—"

I stopped him with a gesture, palms out toward him. "We can argue for half an hour, and then get to the questions," I said, "or we can get to the questions. If you're in a hurry, I suggest cutting the argument part of it."

Another enormous sigh. "Knave, man, why won't you just let us do our work?"

"Because I've got to do mine," I said. "Maybe you don't have to talk to me too long—a lot of what I need is probably going to be in your files on the case. And other cases."

Yeager put in: "He wants the files. He wants us to open up the files." There was blank astonishment in his tone. I nodded at him, affably.

"Exactly right," I said. "It would save the Hell of a lot of everybody's time."

Of course, it wasn't that simple—it never is.

But after fifteen minutes or so of discussion, the last part of which was a list of the first few questions I had to ask, Gross heaved one last sigh and levered himself up off his chair.

"Files," he said. "You wait here. I'll get you files, Knave. You can read them right here—Terry's out, so just use that desk." He pointed at the desk nearest the door. "I'll have the damn stuff printed out. It will not leave this building. It will not even leave this God damned room."

"Ramsay Leake, and a little more," I said. "Those Berigot, five years ago—"

"Oh, dear God," Gross said. "You're still onto that?"

I nodded. He went past me to the door.

"There's going to be a large pile of it," he said.

"That's all right," I told him, with a certain amount of resignation. "I've got time."

TWENTY-TWO

THE FILES ON the Berigot shootings five years before turned out to be extensive. Gross came back with a sizable, indeed massive, printout which, he told me, was the contents and summary list for the files, not the files themselves. "You want to go through the whole thing, it ought to take you four or five days," he said. "But you did tell us you had time."

"Is there a quicker way?" I said, hoping for the right answer.

I didn't get it, not right away. Gross said: "Not for us."

"I'll tell the First Files people how helpful you're being," I said. "And B'russ'r."

Gross, who had gone back to his desk after piling the absent Terry's to incredible heights with faxprint paper, heaved a gigantic sigh. "You're truly determined to make my life miserable, aren't you, Knave?" he said.

"Not really," I said. "Just a small bit of it. And you can probably help make even that bit smaller. If you know the story on the Berigot shootings, tell me. B'russ'r and First Files will give you gold stars."

"They wouldn't give me an eyeblink if I dropped down dead right here at this desk," Gross said. "But I know the story–Lord, after you two pounded away at a connection, I went back and looked, all over again. Just to make sure I hadn't forgotten something vital, you know–it's been five years."

"But a Beri doesn't get shot every day of the week," I said. "A thing like that would stick in your memory."

"It did that," he said. "We worked it, all three of them, for everything we had. Believe it."

"For instance," I said, and he was off.

* * *

THE FIRST BERI shot–G'ril Mnus, attached to the Manuscript Division as Chief Collator, Twentieth-Century–had been taking a night flight near her residence, on the outskirts of City Two. There was a Beri colony out to the North of the city proper, and G'ril lived alone, in one of the fancier nests or perches or whatever the Hell they are. I've seen them, and been invited into one of them, and this language I'm trying to use doesn't have a word for them—never having needed one, because people don't live like that.

It doesn't matter just what the place was, in any case, because she wasn't in it. She'd felt the way I feel when I want to stretch my legs, only more so—as near as I can make it out. And she'd gone out to do a little swooping and diving, sailplaning around the neighborhood. Maybe stopping in to visit a friend, or drop into a neighborhood bar.

They do have bars, more or less. Within reason. If you're not too fussy about definitions.

She was about four hundred yards from her place—just a step outside, to a sailplaning Beri—when something tore her right wing. She went into a ragged dive and tried to smooth it out for landing, but the wing wouldn't grab air; she spun out of control and just did manage to bounce down, first on a tree-branch (oak, if it matters) and then on the local grass. A few bruises, but nothing really serious, and that result was good luck and good sailplaning, both. G'ril was middle-aged by Beri standards—about thirty Standard years, but Beri years are shorter; the average life-span for Berigot, in Standard years, is about fifty-five—and in the sort of shape a regularly jogging human might be in at forty or so, given good habits, good diet and fine genes. A sailplaning expert, among Berigot, is about as odd as a jogging expert might be among people—people jog, and some jog better than others, and some can offer tips to newcomers, but that's about it—but if there were such a thing as an Expert rating, G'ril would have had it.

Whether her shooter knew that, or cared, nobody had any notion.

What had torn a hole in G'ril's right wing was a projectile of some sort. Careful examination, first in the local hospital's Berigot wards and then by a small troop of police experts, fined that down to "small projectile", and the force seemed to say slug gun rather than, say, blowgun dart.

It was quickly established that G'ril was going to live, and that with some patching she'd get most of the use of her wing back. She'd "limp" a little, but she'd be able to get around, and some sailplaning would still be possible, after a spell of rehab. (She did change jobs—the rehab took time, and there was some reshuffling, and she ended in a wing devoted to Early

Comity Settlements—but though her life had changed, it was not a total ruin.) While this was getting itself established, of course, police were out in force hunting for that small projectile.

They had even more surprising luck than G'ril had had in her landing: they found the damn thing. Buried in the upper trunk of another oak, maybe fifteen feet from where she'd been when shot, and a little higher from the ground than G'ril said she had been at the time.

The bullet track—it was a bullet, of course, and from a slug gun, and probably (we could now say) from the same gun that had killed Ramsay Leake—wasn't very deep, but it gave the police an inkling of an angle of fire, and the height of the bullet-hole, the estimated height of G'ril when shot (and if it's a fact, a Beri is trustworthy on it) and the distance from tree to scene of disaster, gave a better one. The shooter had, apparently, been on the ground, behind a small hedge, firing up into the night sky at a sailplaning Beri.

Not as difficult as it sounds, given even a fairly cheap night scope. But the distance involved argued for a fairly powerful gun, and the bullet, though too deformed to be much of a help, argued the same.

There were two lines of inquiry: enemies or rivals of G'ril Mnus, and evidence around that hedge. Neither line led anywhere in particular; G'ril's Enemies list was as tiny as most Berigot lists are—they're not much on personal relationships, of course, and professional rivalry among Berigot doesn't seem to exist. They do whatever it is they do, each one of them, and, since any position anywhere affords endless chances of collecting information, they don't jostle each other to get better positions.

The ground around the hedge offered some scuffs and traces that might have been footprints and might have been almost anything else. No handy wrappers from things carelessly dropped, no cigarette butts stamped out nearby, no lovely thread of jacket or pants or skirt or sock caught in the hedge or anywhere nearby.

This argued a certain amount of care and thought on the part of the shooter, but not necessarily very much; it might be he was just the neat type, and didn't smoke or eat snacks, at least not while waiting to get off a shot.

Was the shooter human, or Beri? Gross, and everybody else, opted for human, on no better ground than that Berigot didn't do things like that;

inventing a motive for one Beri to shoot another is an exhausting and fruitless business.

The investigation went on through about two pounds of printout, but the sketch you've just had covers it; the rest is confirming detail.

The second shooting, twenty-two days later, was an entirely different kettle of mania.

TWENTY-THREE

THE TARGET AND victim was G'mancae B'dint, and G'mancae was a Figure of Importance. He was, in fact, B'russ'r's boss, and G'ril's as well—the Beri-liaison head of Berigot Services for First Files Building itself.

He was elderly, as Berigot go—fifty-two Standard years old. He'd been working for the library most of his adult life, and knew the building and its contents almost as well as the building computers. He was respected among the Berigot, for his knowledge and for his willingness to share it with anyone who might ask, and among human beings for the same qualities, plus a natural friendliness that was far from a common Beri trait, to the degree he showed it. People liked G'mancae, and he seemed (insofar as a Beri could have emotions about anything but data) to like them.

He'd been working that day, and as Berigot will he'd taken a short break to sailplane around the building. It's the Beri equivalent of the trip to the water-dispenser, really—a fifteen-minute-or-so swoop here and there, and then a return to the demands of the day.

He took the break just before three in the afternoon—fifteen, if you insist—opened a window and got out on the perch; and took off. He was considering a small change in a stack system for some late-Twentieth magazines—an ordering change that might, he thought, clarify some relationships among the magazines, that (he considered) hadn't got enough attention. Still considering, he did a fast bank around the side of the building, toward the rear, riding a handy wind current up fifty feet or so and approaching the top of the building.

The ordering change left him as he sailplaned; in the air, a Beri seems to have very little complex thought. Cares drop away, and all sorts of ravel'd sleeves are knit up. He'd given himself up to the joys of sailplaning almost entirely when his left wing was ripped open.

G'mancae wasn't as lucky as G'ril had been; the shock froze him, and he dropped like a stone, whirling helplessly. As he neared the ground (he said later) he tried to control the fall with his right wing, but he didn't have time or room by then. He hit the greensward on his back, at an angle.

The impact broke several of the radiating bones that serve Berigot as basic support instead of a spinal column. There was a burst of pain, and he lost consciousness.

A human—Paul Antrim, working in the stacks—happened to be at a water-dispenser on the third floor, and looking out a window. He saw G'mancae drop past him, and rushed out of doors. It was Antrim who called out others, and got emergency med help to the scene; G'mancae was lying in a hospital hammock, still unconscious, within thirty minutes of his fall.

They'd taken every possible precaution, but though the broken bones eventually healed, there had been nerve damage that couldn't be repaired; G'mancae's left wing was not going to be usable again. Most of the damage had come in the fall; the wing itself, and the tendon and nerve systems underlying it, were as patchable as G'ril's had been; but the fall had snapped controlling nerves in the back, and for Berigot those nerves don't regenerate.

That was a tragedy, and a tragedy of sizable proportions; a Beri who can't sailplane is prone to every sort of melancholia and depression. But G'mancae fought back, and took a post, a couple of months later, as consultant to First Files, a much less demanding job, and managed to rebuild his life.

The police had less success. Gross was beginning to feel very frustrated, he told me, and I could sympathize: at first glance, the shooting of G'mancae had looked like a break.

There was never any serious question whether the two shootings were connected; of course they were. Two Berigot, shot with slug guns, within a month of each other, would have been one of those coincidences people tell reverent stories about, if they hadn't been connected. And this one was in daylight, in a nice public place—people were always going in and out of First Files, and the building had enough windows to stock your average small city.

But people weren't, it seemed, always going in and out of the *back* of the library building—there weren't any doors back there. Just a sort of small greenflower greensward, with some scattered trees and walking-trees in the middle distance, a hundred yards or so away. It was occasionally used as a picnic area by people connected with the building, but not that day—of course.

And the windows weren't exactly mined with spies and sentries. People in libraries are reading books, as a rule—or consulting files, or some such damn thing. They will occasionally glance out a window for a few seconds, if only to rest their eyes by changing focus; but in all of Grand Central Library, exactly one (1) set of eyes, Paul Antrim's, had seen G'mancae fall. And nobody had seen his shooter.

It became even more obvious that the shooter hadn't been seen when police scoured the greensward for clues: footprints, cigarette butts, dropped wrappers (well, maybe this time) and the like. They found only one usable clue there, but that was the bullet itself—in the greenflower, about a hundred and ten feet from the building.

Further from it than G'mancae had been.

The Beri had been shot either from a window of First Files, or from the roof. The windows were eliminated—not quickly, because the Hell of a lot of library workers, library visitors and the occasional tourist had to be questioned, but very thoroughly, and very completely.

But things looked even more hopeful then, for a brief while: the building had had a finite number of people in it or coming through it anywhere around the critical time, a number smaller than the population of City Two (which was the basic pool of suspects for the G'ril shooting—plus tourists and travelers), and after all, who could get up on the roof?

The answer to that question turned out to be, unfortunately: Anybody at all. There were no guards, and no locks; the roof was reachable by a staircase from the top floor, and a convenient trap door. When you thought about it, why the Hell would there have been locks, or guards either? The building sat by itself in the middle of a greenflower grassland; there was nothing valuable sitting on the roof; and even a suicide would find a higher building more attractive as a jumping-off spot: First Files was a lousy six stories high, even though the stories were sizable—like most libraries, the place had high ceilings.

And careful examination of the roof turned up nothing in particular. There was one thing—a thread of cloth that had got itself snagged by a rough spot on a 3V piping up there. But it didn't lead anywhere in particular. It might have been up there for days, and people did use the roof now and then just as they used the surrounding grassland.

There was a full report on the thread. Cotton, hothouse-grown on Ravenal—which meant it was expensive, and comparatively uncommon though not really rare—dyed dark blue, and treated against shrinkage, fading and, I suppose, warts. Jackets, pants, jumpers, skirts, blouses or dresses of that material in that color were worn by perhaps fifty thousand people in City Two.

Who had been wearing clothing made of that material, that day, in that building? The file got a little vague just there; lots of people simply didn't remember. Ravenal is not a clothes-horse sort of place, and cross-checking to find out if people remembered what *other* people had been wearing was even less helpful. The thread hadn't been turned up till three days after the shooting—it took two to find out that the roof ought to be looked at—and nobody really expected results better than that.

There was a list of ten people who had definitely been wearing something made of that material, and six more probables. None of them was a name I recognized, but I filed them all, of course, and made a note to ask the Master and little Robbin what, if anything, they knew about these sixteen; it was perfectly possible that they knew more than the police did, even after police investigation. Or at the very least knew different things.

And the police investigation had been very thorough—and, after a while, very frantic. One of those sixteen, after all, was a shining candidate for the post of Berigot Maimer—the election being clouded some by the fact that there might have been others wearing the material, and by the fact that six of the sixteen were only probable, not certain, for it. Not to mention the fact that nobody was anything like positive that the thread had been left on the roof on that particular day.

Nothing of any interest turned up.

Two and a half weeks went by.

Then, at eleven o'clock of an especially dark night (as dark as the night of the theft, five years further along)—twenty-three if you're following this Scientifically—somebody shot B'dyr G'ridget. B'dyr was just returning home from a visit with friends—human friends, as it happens—and was about a hundred and fifty feet from his nest-or-whatever, on the outskirts of a Berigot area (not the area G'ril lived in), and about forty feet in the air.

He was hit in the left wing, managed to brake his fall a bit, and landed without serious incident.

I could detail it for you, but what's the use? Gross and a stack of printout detailed it for me, and it was all one large zero. Happily, B'dyr wasn't hurt, except for the damaged wing, which was repairable. He had a few bumps and bruises, and was out of the office for a couple of days–he worked as a text analyst in Early Comity, and did some work in the late-Twentieth offices down the hall–but he got away, comparatively speaking, without a scratch.

He was, at 28 Standard, the youngest of the three victims. Did that mean anything?

Did *anything* mean anything?

According to Gross and the printouts, the answer was: God knows. Certainly God knows; that's His business. But nobody else does.

And as of even date and time, nobody else did.

TWENTY-FOUR

GROSS AND I had spent an exhausting afternoon, and so had the mechs who had printed out all the reports. Thanking the mechs was impossible, and thanking Gross didn't seem sufficient, but it was all I had to hand out. He took the thanks with tired grace, and I left the office, and the building, sped home and got on the phone.

Master Higsbee had heard of one of the sixteen names, and heard quite a lot. He was vaguely familiar with nine others, but it was that one that got his attention—and, therefore, positively clutched at mine.

"Geraint Beauthis," he said reflectively. "An odd person, Gerald. He was once arrested for failure to comply—I cannot recall the object of compliance, but it must have been fairly serious at the time; the usual procedure in noncompliance is a simple warning and an oversight long enough to ensure compliance. I remember it as being perhaps six years in the past."

"That makes him odd?" I said. "There are several hundred things I don't comply with, or wouldn't. Several thousand."

"Few of an importance sufficient to cause arrest," the Master said. "And you do not normally reside on Ravenal, Gerald. Compliance is very general here; few wish to invest time or energy in unusual social stances, if they require battle with the law."

"If you say so," I said. "Can you scare up details on this Beauthis? And on the other nine?"

"I shall do so," the Master said. "And inquire of Robbin Tress as well, when I can speak with her—tomorrow morning will be the earliest possible time. Is there anything else?"

"Well—" I said, trying to think if there was.

"Finished," the Master said after half a second.

Click.

Well, there probably hadn't been.

* * *

AN ODD QUESTION had found its way into my head, and after I'd put the phone down I started to look at it.

Someone had gone to a great deal of trouble to turn out an awfully convincing forgery. Why?

The usual reason for committing a forgery is money: if somebody believes the thing you've put together is really by Chaucer, or Julius Verne, or Heinlein, or some such famous corpse, he may pay through any and all available noses to own it.

But the manuscript of *The Stone Pillow* had never been offered for sale, not for a second, and nobody had ever thought it might have been. Once dug up, it was going straight to First Files Building, to be treasured as an artifact, displayed as a wonder, and even guarded fairly well. There was no money in it whatever—if you except the additional fees paid by tourists and scholars interested in coming into the library to see the manuscript.

Somehow, that teeny pittance—and it was teeny; fees were paid to the usual mechs, to enter the library, and to examine some special areas (including late-Twentieth manuscripts), but they were very small indeed; the fee paid on entrance, for instance, wouldn't be enough to buy a cup of coffee and a pastry anywhere in City Two—somehow, that didn't seem like enough motive for the work that had had to be involved.

But the work had been done, and there was *The Stone Pillow*. And—well, *why* was it?

It struck me that I had two complementary puzzles on my hands:

1. Why was Ping so damned anxious to recover what was essentially a worthless forgery?

2. Why had anyone ever *constructed* what was essentially a worthless forgery—a job without any pay in it I could see?

Were these two questions related? I worked away at answers to that for a while.

Suppose (I said to myself) the forgery was really only a cover for some secret message, meant for Ping himself? The whole business of making the forgery and getting it into the library might have been a cover for getting some very complicated secret message to Ping by a channel no one would ever suspect.

I was very fond of that answer; it was showy as all Hell, and so beautifully complex, when you started to examine it, that it set new records for my head. Unfortunately, it was also nonsense.

I couldn't come up with any reason for Ping not to have read the message, acted on it, or at the very least either memorized it or copied it, some time during the four years the manuscript had been lying around the place. And if he'd done any of those things, then recovering the manuscript itself was a meaningless exercise.

He'd have had to go through the motions, of course—call in the police, look worried and so on. But Gerald Knave, if you'll pardon an obvious truth, was not one of the motions he'd have had to go through; Gerald Knave was a special expense, and a very expensive special expense (though not, I reflected, nearly expensive enough; what with the longueurs of bargaining, he seldom is). Calling me in meant that Ping had seriously wanted the manuscript back.

I tried to come up with a message that couldn't be copied or memorized in four years. After much thought, my head returned me an answer: There ain't no such animal.

But it also returned me another thought. The forgery was of a Heinlein manuscript—the most loved, the most valued, of all science-fiction writers from before the Clean Slate War.

Was its appearance designed, perhaps, to smoke out secret sf fans? I knew how carefully Mac and the others guarded their hobby, or interest, or mania, or whatever it was. Could the forgery have been meant to force them into public avowals?

Again, it was a perfectly lovely idea, and again it made no sense. Charles Darwin, my Classical education told me, had once defined a tragedy as: "A beautiful theory, killed by a nasty, ugly little fact." The nasty, ugly little f. this time around was that the appearance of *The Stone Pillow* had done nothing whatever to make any sf fans anywhere go public, and there was no reason to believe that it ever could have. Other manuscripts, even other manuscripts by Heinlein, existed in the library. *The Stone Pillow* had had no more effect on the public actions of sf fans on Ravenal than the other manuscripts had had—and there was no reason why it ever should have. It was a surprise, an unknown Heinlein story—but nobody could think that even that surprise would push sf fans into the open. They could go to First Files Building and check the thing out, just from natural curiosity, without really giving themselves away; and they had.

I shuffled the data around in my head for a little while, and came up with two statements:

1. Somebody had gone to the Hell of a lot of trouble, for no purpose I could figure out.

2. I had been hired to go to the Hell of a lot of trouble, for no purpose I could figure out.

This was a simple, even a charming picture. That it made no sense was, in a way, a plus: things do not, in the actual world, make that little sense.

I was, in other words, missing a fact, possibly sixty-seven facts, that would assort this simple picture into a sensible one.

Maybe, I told myself with a certain amount of idiotic hope, Geraint Beauthis would provide one or more of them, when the Master and Robbin Tress got around to digging up a dossier on him and passing it on to me.

Anything, after all, was possible.

So I stacked everything neatly in my head, put it in the care of whoever it is lives in the back of my head where the real work always gets done, and went out for dinner.

This turned out to be something of a mistake.

TWENTY-FIVE

I picked the place almost at random. I was busily trying new restaurants throughout my stay in City Two, looking for one that had the capability to become a regular stop while I was on planet; the Rose & Corona hadn't been bad, away back before I'd even met Ping Boom, but the track record of City Two since then had not been anything to keep as a souvenir. I'd done a good deal better with my own cooking—which is not all that rare a fact. But I still had hopes, and a place called the Art Café seemed to promise well; cookery is, after all, an art.

Nor was I wholly disappointed; the chef there seemed to understand a few things about a dish I'm fond of, eggplant parmigiana (as I may have said once or twice, I have low tastes; it is not ever a gourmet specialty, which is a loss only to gourmets); he had the sense to serve it with spaghetti bolognese (I have known places to serve it with a baked potato and a salad, but I have not known them more than once each), and somewhere on Ravenal somebody had made a loving career out of providing fresh parmesan to grate onto the spaghetti. With a decent wine, and decent coffee, it would have made an admirable dinner for a single fellow far from his usual haunts.

Well, you can't have everything, and some days you can't even have a terribly high percentage of thing. The wine was wine the way the Blackjack beer had been beer, only even less so; and the coffee had been brewed from the ground bits of a bean that somehow resembled the coffee bean, but not very much.

And it was not, as things turned out, a dinner for a single fellow at all; it was a dinner for a man accompanied by two sf fans.

Corri Reges and Chandes Washington, whom I'd met and talked to at some length back at the Misfits affair, had been having a little dinner of their own in a corner just dim enough so that I didn't notice them when I came in and found my own table. But Corri noticed me, and within bare minutes had trundled her wide little self on over to ask if she and her dark, thin and baritone companion could join me.

Well, why not? Given a little time and wine, I might even be able to think up a question or two worth asking. And how much of a disturbance could either of them be to my digestion?

Don't ask.

Of course, whether or not I had questions, Corri did. Who had stolen the manuscript, and was I going to catch up to the thief in minutes, or was it going to take hours? I said my conclusions and plans were confidential, because the library wanted them that way (whether or not Ping did, I did; the way to handle back-seat drivers is to remove the back seat). I tried to look as confident as humanly possible while I was saying that, and Chandes Washington nodded gravely at me.

"The library," he said. "You do mean First Files Building."

"Well, actually," I said, "I meant the people in it. Just careless of me, calling a public collection of books and manuscripts a library."

Corri giggled. I have no idea why wide women, or round women, giggle more than thin ones. It could be that, because they eat more, on average, they're happier. "We have simple names for things here," she said. "We do understand that they confuse outsiders—we take no offense at it."

"But why would they want everything kept quiet?" Chandes said. He still looked as if he'd got lost somehow many years ago, and hadn't yet found a way back to anywhere in particular. But his wide-opened eyes were sharp. "I should think—now the story of the theft is pretty well out—they'd want to publicize any success."

"Mine not to reason why," I said casually. "They pay the piper, they call the tune." I had not lied so often in so few words in some time, but Chandes nodded.

"I suppose so," he said. "They're a bit odd over there in any case, always have been. Comes of associating with Beris, I think."

Corri said: "Berigot, Chan."

"Berigot," he said. "Whatever. There's something—disturbing about them. Bothersome."

Corri giggled again. "Me," she said, "I think they're cute."

The idea of a cute B'russ'r B'dige stopped me for a second, but I nodded and smiled at her. "They do fine work for First Files Building, I understand," I said. "Great librarians."

Chandes snorted, and swallowed some wine to soothe irritated passages—he and Corri were having some sort of marinara angel-hair fish fry, and had been supplied with a bottle of the house white, a common error even with decent wine: fish or beef, tomato sauce calls for a red and a hearty one. "What kind of librarians can they be?" he said. "How can they understand the culture they must deal with?"

I shrugged. "They seem to do all right with it," I said. "I haven't heard many complaints."

Another snort, another swallow and a refilled glass. "People are too polite to complain," he said flatly. "Mustn't upset the poor Beris' feelings, you know. Not at all the nice thing to do."

"Berigot," Corri said. "Chan, honestly—"

"I'm entitled to my opinion," Chandes said, turning to her. It was almost a waspish snap, which assorts very oddly with a deep baritone voice. "Even in City Two. Even these days."

I knew what he meant by "these days". There's a sort of irregular cycle some societies go through. For a while they're relaxed and comfortable with whatever the rules of the society are—and for this cycle, it doesn't much matter what rules I'm talking about; anything that will last forty or fifty Standard years will do for a set.

Then, for another while, they begin to get nervous. They begin insisting on the rules—all the rules. The small social rules become very big social rules, and sometimes legal rules. The personal rules become social rules. Everything gets very tense.

(Oddly, at this point in the cycle the legal rules relax, quite a lot. It is felt to be unkind to enforce them fully. There may be a point to that feeling; when the social and personal rules are being so tightly enforced, any society has to find some relaxation somewhere. If it becomes less and less possible to use rude names, say, there may be a point to making it more and more possible to steal small objects.)

City Two—a large fraction of Ravenal generally, in fact—was going through a tense period. It had been possible, once upon a time, to dislike Berigot—or human beings—or bald men, or redheaded women. Now, it almost wasn't. The social rule of personal equality was being enforced tightly. It would relax again—it always does—but in the meantime people with opinions like Chandes Washington's were being made to feel uncomfortable.

Nothing serious or useful was being done to change their opinions. But everybody felt highly moral about their discomfort.

Corri said, gently and soothingly: "Of course you are, Chan. Everybody is entitled to any opinion, we all know that. But you have to show some courtesy."

Two errors in one speech, both of them due to the phase of the societal cycle the place was in, so I didn't point them out.

a) The people who are entitled to an opinion on any subject are the people who have taken the trouble to have some grasp of the subject. Invitations are not issued to others; and shouldn't be.

b) Courtesy to Berigot is shown in the presence of Berigot—none of whom inhabited the Art Café, or were likely to in the usual course of a week, say, food requirements for humans and Berigot being as different as they are. Courtesy to human beings who might not share Chandes Washington's opinion of Berigot is shown by fairly polite speech—which he'd had, more or less. Not by shutting up about the opinion; or no one would ever be able to express any opinion whatever, for fear of being discourteous to someone nearby who might disagree with it.

I took in some more eggplant, swallowed some wine-or-whatever, and settled myself for a long period of not saying much. The sort of discussion Corri and Chandes had begun can go on for several weeks before the Chandes wing wears out its indignation, or the Corri wing wears out its highly superior loving-kindness. But this time, other factors came into play.

"Whatever you call them," Chandes said suddenly, in reply to something from Corri I hadn't properly heard—having so arranged my ears—"they're odd, and they make the people in First Files Building odd, too. They were going around, just a few weeks ago, asking questions about someone who didn't even work there. No connection with the place at all. I happened to be there on the argon search—you know about that, Corri?"

"Naturally occurring isotopes, surprisingly long lives, as traces in the atmosphere of Kingsley," Corri Reges said, and nodded. I opened my mouth to ask six or seven questions—I'd never heard of argon isotopes, though I'd been on Kingsley once or twice—when Chandes said:

"That's right. Some fellow called Beauthis."

"Never heard of him," Corri said. "I suppose there must be a reason of some kind—"

I was leaning forward, perilously close, as I noticed two entire minutes later, to my handy mound of spaghetti. "Beauthis?" I said carefully. Perhaps I'd misheard; it isn't the simplest name in the world to pronounce.

"Gerald Beauthis," Chandes said. "Or Garand."

"Geraint," I said, and he nodded.

"Oh," he said. "Is this part of your investigation? I hadn't thought so, because no one mentioned your name at all. They might have been from the late-Twentieth department, though, I do remember that one of them seemed vaguely familiar. A young girl of some sort."

Ignoring the question of just how many sorts of young girls there might altogether prove to be in the universe, I said: "It's all news to me, but I am interested. What were they asking?"

Chandes shrugged. "Something about concealed weapons," he said. "They didn't ask me much at all, because I hadn't been there the previous Fourday, which is apparently when this Beauthis had been there, or been thought to have been there, or some such. And I wasn't paying any sort of close attention—" How many sorts of close attention can be paid was another question I was willing to let slide right on by—"to what they asked any of the others. I had my own work to do."

"By the way," Corri said, "how is that coming? Is there actually a trace of such a thing? Occurring in nature?"

"Well," Chandes said, and I broke in:

"I'd really like to hear about this Beauthis matter, if you don't mind."

Very impolite, and so probably outlawed by current social tensions.

Very unhelpful, too, because that was all Chandes Washington knew, and Corri Reges, when asked, didn't even know that much, and had never, she told me, so much as heard the name Geraint Beauthis before.

Damn.

A frustrating evening, all in all, made more so by the fact that I never did learn anything more about naturally occurring, long-lived isotopes of argon, which are definitely supposed not to exist, and apparently do, at least on Kingsley.. The discussion eventually veered from Geraint Beauthis to someone named Bobathic, who worked in Third Artifact Building, and whose name Corri was reminded of by Beauthis', and who had said something exceptionally nasty about Berigot the week before. She was using him as a horrible example to change Chandes Washington's impolite ways, which didn't work very well but took up a great deal of time and air, and the discussion sank right on back to its previous level, with indignation and loving-kindness fighting it out to a wholly predictable, and very distant, draw. I contributed a few small noises of comprehension and politeness here and there, and made mental notes on questions I was going to want to ask Ping Boom and B'russ'r B'dige and anyone else I could find over at the library.

After a long while, dinner was over, and I declined an invitation from Corri to accompany them on a walk through Bohr Park, which was nearby. They went off, and I went off, and I spent the night making up lists of questions.

Concealed weapons?

TWENTY-SIX

THE NEXT MORNING, bright and shockingly early—the library opened at nine, and I was actually at the door ten minutes before that—I began trying to get some answers. Even the first few turned out to be surprisingly hard to get.

The trouble was to find someone who knew the answers. This should have been easy—and if I'd started with Ping Boom or B'russ'r it almost certainly would have been. What I ran into, instead, was a an eager young fellow called Reddin Corrosopie, and Reddin was something just a hair special.

I was a little early for Ping, and didn't want to bother B'russ'r with what was basically a single simple question: what had been the story on Geraint Beauthis and the concealed weapon? The library people—all right, the people of First Files Building, but I'll try not to have to say it again—had made a very public business of asking around, and the bare bones of the story couldn't very well have been a state secret anywhere.

Reddin Corrosopie was the Public Information clerk. Naturally, since this was Ravenal, they didn't call him that. There was a sign over his desk, which was near the entrance where a mech had just swallowed my paltry coins for the entrance fee—a tasteful big thing, that said: *First Files: Facts.* But I got the idea, and ambled over to try my luck.

Reddin, I think, knew his name and the name of the building he was in. Otherwise—well, to say he didn't have a clue is to flatter him with a butter-trowel. Reddin had never known a clue. He had never met a clue. He had never so much as sent a clue an anonymous Christmas card.

I introduced myself: "I'm Gerald Knave." He looked at me with a perfectly blank little face, as handsome as a painting and as full of motion.

"Yes?"

It's a response I have always had trouble with. I said: "Yes. I'm Gerald Knave. I'd like to ask you about Geraint Beauthis."

"The author listings are in Catalog B," he said. "Just to your left as you go straight ahead."

"He's not an author," I said. "He was here the other week. There was a charge—concealed weapons in the building. I'd like to know about it."

Reddin Corrosopie blinked at me. "He's not an author?"

I shook my head. "Not as far as I know," I said. "He was here, and there was a charge against him. I'd like to know what happened."

He took a deep breath and frowned. "It seems to me," he said slowly, in a flute-like voice, "that *you're* telling *me* what happened. You said he was here and concealed something. Library property, perhaps. But that would be someone else's desk. You might try Security."

I took one myself. "I intend to try Security," I said. "But I'd like to know just a little about what I'm trying first, if I can. Do you know what date he was here, and what the charge was, exactly?"

"What date who was here?" this Corrosopie said.

I should have wished him a good day and traded elsewhere. But I have a stubborn streak, and now and then it surfaces. "Geraint Beauthis."

He blinked at me. He had large eyes that bugged out just a little, and a pale, almost transparent complexion. "The author?" he said.

"Author of what?" I said, and he told me, as I should certainly have known he was going to:

"The author listings are in Catalog B. Just to your left as you go straight ahead."

"No," I said. "Geraint Beauthis. The man who was here, in this building, the other week, and was charged with illegal weapons possession. It can't happen very often; you must have heard something about it at the time."

He blinked again. He combed long, thin fingers through his sparse blond hair. "Oh," he said. "The man with the catapult."

It was my turn to blink, not to mention gape. "The what?"

"The man," he said. I took a deep breath.

"The man with the what?"

"Oh," he said. "Catapult. You mean him."

"It begins to look as if I might," I said. "There was a man here with a catapult?" A catapult can certainly be a weapon; back in the preSpace Middle Ages people used to toss everything from boiling tar to flaming mattresses over castle walls by means of the things. But it had then been a rig eight or nine feet high and correspondingly broad, and weighing upwards of a ton. It was hard to imagine anyone at all trucking one past the library doors and into a reading room, and even harder to imagine him concealing one, even from the penetrating, if slightly bulging, eyes of Reddin Corrosopie.

"He had one in his pocket," this Corrosopie said. "Security thought he might damage something with it."

I revised my mental picture. Clearly there was such a thing as a small, or model, catapult, suitable for carrying around in a handy pocket. "Do you know when it happened?"

"In the afternoon," he told me.

I sighed. "The afternoon of what particular day, would you happen to remember?"

"I don't have to remember," he said. "Security will have it all listed."

"Right," I said. "It's Security's listing I'm after. But it would be nice to know what day to tell them to check for it."

"Fourday," he said, "three weeks ago. Or four weeks ago. I think it was Fourday, some day like that."

It seemed to me likely that Threeday would be a day like that. Or Sixday. Eightday wouldn't be a day like that only because Ravenal had no such thing as an Eightday. I sighed once more.

"You're sure about the catapult?" I said.

"Sure, I'm sure," Reddin Corrosopie told me. "I don't forget things very easily."

I let that pass. I let almost everything pass, in fact, and asked him if he had heard about someone called Gerald Knave, who had been hired by Ping Boom of Manuscripts to work for First Files Building on a special assignment. I made it as detailed and thorough a question as I could manage.

"Oh, that," he said. "That's got nothing to do with this fellow who had the catapult. Sure I heard about Mr. Knave."

"I'm Gerald Knave," I said. "I mentioned that before, but you were thinking of something else at the time."

"I was?" he said.

I nodded. "You were," I said firmly. "And I'd like one bit of information from you."

"Oh, sure, Mr. Knave," he said.

I asked him for the code for First Files Building event retrieval, and he gave it to me. He directed me to a query room where, he told me, one bank of computers would accept that code. He told me which bank, and how to find it.

Everything he told me was accurate. I have seldom been so surprised.

* * *

EVENT RETRIEVAL GAVE me the basic story; I keyed in *Geraint Beauthis* and *catapult* and let the thing hunt, and in about four seconds it stopped humming, clicked, and asked me did I want a print, or would I take the data on screen? I told it to go right ahead and print, and in a minute or so more it spat out three sheets of fax paper at me. I thanked the thing politely, shut it off, and went away to read and reflect. Something, I felt, did not make sense; which made this piece of the puzzle, if it was actually a piece of the same puzzle, just like almost all the other pieces.

I'll leave off routing and access codes and the like, about a page of numbers, letters and symbols, all told:

* * *

NOTIFICATION REPORT:

Mr. Geraint Beauthis (1122-067-ABN6Px, GP file AV194) notified this day that carrying a weapon concealed in First Files Building without specific permit is an offense. Notifiers: Ptl. Harra Gleme, Ptl. 2 Rob Alan Deniende.

Weapon: 1 catapult, pocket version. Reported to be in left pocket jacket, report accurate.

Armament for catapult, steel pellets 1/4 inch diam, 30, found in right pocket jacket.

WEAPON SPECIFICATIONS: See p 3

RATIONALE GIVEN: Mr. Beauthis had purchased catapult as gift for birthday of a nephew. He took possession without packaging, to allow ease of transport. Catapult was fired twice in shop where purchased (Maxim's Objects) as test of mechanism, accuracy and range. Mr. Beauthis did not intend firing catapult in building, or at any other location.

RATIONALE CHECK: Made.

RATIONALE A/R: Accepted.

DISPOSITION: Mr. Beauthis was formally notified. He undertakes to deposit any future weapons with First Files Facts clerk on duty if transporting weapon within building.

* * *

EVERYBODY HAS NEPHEWS, and everybody buys toys for them. The youngster might put some school chum's eye out with his new rig, but that was his worry, and the chum's, and perhaps Geraint Beauthis'; it wasn't mine.

Damn.

TWENTY-SEVEN

A THOROUGHLY WASTED couple of hours, all in all. I spent some time trying to fit a toy catapult into a plot to break into the damn building to get the Heinlein forgery, and came up with nothing much. I spent some more time trying to figure out if a toy catapult could fire a slug, ready-deformed, with enough force and at a long enough range to have fooled the local police, and came up with two answers: a) Almost certainly not, unless it were one Hell of a powerful toy, and b) Even if so, why in the name of God would anybody want to do such a thing, when slug guns were, after all, not frighteningly hard to lay hold of?

Not that this process of thought eliminated Geraint Beauthis from consideration as a possible player. After all, forgers and thieves have nephews, too, and doubtless buy their nephews toys now and then.

But I will not deny that it was a disappointment. I never had any doubt of the tale as told to me by the event retrieval computer; if the building cops said they had checked things out, they had checked things out. I'd had enough experience with the piles of reports on the Beri shootings to trust them for routine of that kind. I did in fact go over to Security and ask them a few questions, and I won't trouble you with any of that, because none of it conflicted in any slightest damn detail with what you've already seen. I made the stop at Security in the interests of thoroughness, and shouldn't have bothered.

I was not, in short, any forwarder at all. Maybe, I told myself, the Master and Robbin would have something nutritious for me to chew on. There had been enough time for him to consult with her, and I scurried back to my apartment and found that my phone-message system was blipping and blinking. Mornings are not my best time, and I'd forgotten to put the thing on transfer page; my pocket piece had never got the news.

I sat down and pushed the Accept button, and the Master said to me, via recording:

"Gerald, call me at once. There is news."

The message beep gave the time as 10:48, nearly two hours before. I cursed, dialed the number, and waited through three blips.

The Master's rasp said: "Who?"

"Gerald Knave," I said.

"Forgetful, Gerald," he said. "You should program transfer page automatically when leaving your phone."

Well, I should. "Yes, Sir," I said.

"I have some data on Geraint Beauthis," he said.

I nodded at the phone. Maybe the Master could get the air pressure changes as my head moved. Or the sound of my head moving. "So have I," I said. "I've been to the Library."

"Ah," he said. "Then you know of the nephew. But my news is other."

"There doesn't seem to be much there," I said. "What have you got?"

"The failure to comply seems interesting, Gerald," the Master said in that rasp. "You may agree."

"Go ahead," I said.

"The subject of compliance was a stock of paper—about half a ream. The paper dates from the mid-twenty-first century, and was manufactured in a small facility near the city of Canberra, on Earth."

I sat holding the phone for a while, thinking about it. The date of the paper was a shade too late to make it useful for the Heinlein forgery, but only a shade—and it had been made on Earth. "Beauthis had this paper?" I said.

"It is the policy of our government to requisition such things," he said. "They serve various purposes—museums, research, testing and so forth. The paper had been held by Mr. Beauthis and his family for generations, and had been well protected for the past hundred years or more." He cleared his throat. You have never heard such a sound. "Mr. Beauthis had never made a great public show of his property, but it had never been wholly secret; the authorities heard of it, and requisitioned it. Mr. Beauthis appears to have been quite vehement in his refusal."

I nodded again. "He felt that the stuff belonged to him," I said. "His property, not the government's."

"Exactly, Gerald," the Master said.

"And he went to prison over half a ream of blank paper?" I said.

"He thought of it as a family heirloom, I believe."

I nodded. "What finally happened?"

"Mr. Beauthis was sentenced to a prison term of two months, and the paper was confiscated." He cleared his throat again. It's not a sound I've ever got used to. You might come close to it by programming an especially noisy sidewalk sweeper, one of the things with wire brushes, to run slowly over a moaning pack of gerbils covered with dry leaves. "He accepted the sentence, which was then commuted to a simple fine and a prison term of three days–quite usual in the case of someone with a job to lose."

"He paid the fine?"

"He did, and has made no trouble since, if we except the business of the catapult."

I thought a little more. "Just what is his job?" I said.

The Master chuckled. "He runs a family business," he said. "A fax-paper manufactory."

I gave that a little silence. "So he might know how to make paper that would pass for mid-Twentieth stock," I said. "Given that he could work the isotope business, of course."

"It is not frighteningly difficult to do so," the Master said. "A competent worker in any one of several fields might be able to do such a job–given materials with the proper isotope assay percentages, of course. But yes, Gerald, he would certainly know how; fax-paper is of course a different material, but there are close manufactory ties."

I reached back into preSpace classical humor for a reply. "Ver-ry interesting."

He gave me his laugh–a single sound that was a cross between chuckle and bark. "I thought you might feel so," he said. "By the way, Gerald, Robbin Tress has some news for you as well, in my talk with her by phone this morning."

"About Geraint Beauthis?" I said.

"I cannot be certain," he said. He gave his laugh again. "She has told me that the ringleader–at any rate, the person who managed the forgery, and also helped to carry out both the forgery and the theft–is someone who has met Gerald Knave."

I stared at the phone. "She what?"

"So she says, " the Master's rasp told me. "Of course, Robbin knows no more than that–she cannot even say whether the person involved is someone you have met recently, or someone you have known for years."

"Right," I said. "If psi powers were dependable–if psi powers are what she's got–my grandmother would have wheels. Or something."

"Exactly, Gerald," he said. "But that is what she now feels, and I pass it to you for what value you may find in it."

TWENTY-EIGHT

I GOT OFF the phone with my head spinning. I now had more facts–from the Library and from Master Higsbee, not to mention little Robbin Tress–if Robbin's feelings were to be accepted as facts, and why the Hell not? They always were facts.

This Beauthis was in the spotlight, that much for certain. I hadn't met him yet, but I was going to meet him very soon if I could manage it, and maybe Robbin's feeling was subject to just a little time slippage.

And if not–I went over the list of people on Ravenal I had met. From Reddin Corrosopie, who was about the most recent, to the landlord of the building I was living in, who was the first person I'd met in more than an official, impersonal way when I'd got to Ravenal this time round.

Then I started adding people I'd met on previous visits. Robbin couldn't tell how long my acquaintance with this X had been, only that there was one. How she knew that, I could not imagine; but my imagination had nothing to do with what was quite definitely a fact. And I had met a lot of people on Ravenal over the years, when I sat down and thought about it for a bit. Jamie Arthur, for instance, with whom I'd had a dinner date a few hours after I'd first been shot at.

But Jamie had no connection I could imagine with this particular case. He was one of the few experts on the society and behavior of one of the odder non-human races around, the Tocks, and we'd spent the evening trading Tock stories, of which there are several thousand worth telling at any given time. I filled him in on some recent doings of their King and Queen, who are old friends of mine, and he filled me in on the latest theories regarding what Tocks knew and how they knew it. They're a highly intelligent race, but they aren't one-tenth as human as the Berigot, and not one-thousandth as understandable.

Full of interest and fascination, and a nice fellow–but no connection. Not a chance.

Mac, for instance. Charles Hutson Bellemand MacDougal—murderer, forger and thief?

Nothing sounded less probable.

On the other hand . . .

Naw.

* * *

THE PUZZLE KEPT growing new pieces. Most puzzles do, as you work at them, but in most cases the pieces do seem to belong to the same puzzle you started with, more or less. In this case, every new piece looked as if it were part of some entirely new puzzle.

This seemed to make for a certain amount of confusion. I spent a little time trying to assort matters reasonably, while cobbling myself up a light lunch of toasted City Four Smoked cheese on large rolls, with thin-sliced onions and tomatoes, and some Kona coffee because Kona married well with the cheese—about which I promised myself I was going to have to find out some more.

The lunch was perfectly satisfactory. The assorting process, even helped along by the calm, contemplative work of doing the dishes, was less so; when I finished I was full, but my head was still empty.

One thing had dawned on me. If Robbin said the main forger and thief was someone I had met on Ravenal, then it was; I could take that to the bank and borrow money on it. But the job had certainly involved more than one person—it would have taken more than one to make up the paper as well as the writing on it, to get the thing somehow into the artifacts once belonging to Norman W. Nechs, and to lift it from the damn library.

Maybe I had only met the ringleader, the General of this very odd campaign. There might be a Colonel or a Major and possibly even a foot-soldier waiting around out there, who could be met at any time.

And maybe I had met a Colonel. God alone knew, for sure.

So I got back to the phone, and began the weary work of finding some of them—or at least finding a few people who looked like candidates for those posts. I'd asked Master Higsbee to inquire after the other members of the final dig team, but he'd been busy inquiring after sixteen other people, not to mention digging into the Leake murder in whatever way he found convenient; he hadn't had time for the dig folk just yet.

But I had time, I had nothing but time. And they weren't at all hard to find; in fact, all three I hadn't yet seen were still, or again, on Ravenal, which was at the very least a handy sort of coincidence. Freda Hocksher was doing a year of teaching at one of the local universities—part of the Scholarte, of course, but I can't recall which part—Lavoisier, I think. Paula Shore had just returned, a week or so before, from another dig, this time somewhere in what used to be Chicago, which had meant (she told me later) a special crew, with underwater equipment of all sorts.

And Grosvenor Rouse was where he usually was, I discovered. Bitsy Bowyer had told me that Gro was really a bit old for digs, though he loved the work, and it seemed that he didn't do much of it any more. He was now full-time, as he had been part-time for some years, Consulting Archaeologist for the damn Library.

Not in the same department as Ping Boom, of course. Not even on the same floor. But right there in the same damn building.

Naturally, I called him first, and he agreed to see me within the hour. I scheduled Paula Shore for the next morning, and Freda Hocksher for the afternoon—all three of the final dig crew were anxious enough to help, once I'd explained what I was asking about, and none of them seemed frantically busied with day-to-day life.

It may be simply that reconstructive archaeologists don't *get* frantically busied like other people. They've learned to take the long view, likely as not.

* * *

GROSVENOR ROUSE HAD an office on the fifth floor of the library, one flight from the top. The office was filled to the brim with Gro Rouse, more printed books than I had seen in one place since I can remember, and what looked like an immense scattering of junk.

Of course it wasn't junk, it was artifacts—some of them nicely preserved in glassex cases, the Hell of a lot of them just scattered over every available surface, collecting dust and fingerprints, I suppose. One or two of the items seemed to be from Alphacent, a world I knew fairly well, but almost all of them looked Earthlike.

There was a computer-reader setup on a desk, almost buried in artifacts and a small blizzard of papers, and there were some chairs scattered around, not many. Gro Rouse took up the rest of the place, and when I came in and shut the door behind me, I felt as if I didn't have the room to take a deep breath.

He was large and round and light-brown—a sort of dusty tan, actually—and essentially hairless, though he'd tried to make up for that with a pair of eyebrows bushy enough to cast shadows. He wore rimless spectacles, old-fashioned as all Hell, and little blue eyes peered at me through the lenses. His mouth looked as if it had once tried to be kind and generous and friendly, and had been severely repressed; he had big lips the color of fresh liver, and, when he smiled, a set of the largest and whitest teeth on the planet. The smile was not worth waiting for, I discovered after a couple of samples; it was quick, big and cold.

His voice was a bass rumble. "You're Knave?" he said as I shut the door.

"Yes, Sir," I said. He reminded me forcibly of a very demanding Professor I'd once had in Tensor Flight Mechanics, and I had to fight to keep from sounding apologetic, about anything at all.

"And you want to discuss this business of the Heinlein manuscript," he said. "Very well, Knave: discuss."

I felt like telling him the dog had eaten my discussion, but I fought the feeling. "It isn't a Heinlein manuscript, Sir," I said.

"Damn it, I know that," Rouse said. "The damned thing is a forgery. A sell. A piece of misdirection. Someone thought—well, who cares about old science-fiction? I can get away with anything here. But they forgot about the isotope patterns, boy. They did indeed."

The Master called me Gerald, and Robbin called me Sir, and now I was being called Boy, which seemed worse than the other two. Rouse was about sixty, so he did edge me by some years—but not enough for Boy; though I'd have taken it without strain from anybody over ninety-three.

"Knave, Sir," I said. "And of course I know about the forgery—that's why I was called in." As an expert, damn it, I nearly added.

"Sure you do," Rouse said. "And so do I, and what the Hell is the problem, boy? I found it, I helped dig it up, it isn't the real thing, and there's an end. No?"

Well—"No," I said. "For you, Sir, the big question is: How did it get there?"

"Get where?" he said. "To the exhibit case? We brought it here, boy. Straight out of its case. A large barrel, if I recall, and I do."

"No, Sir," I said. "How did it get into the large barrel, that's the question. Because it wasn't in existence back when the barrel was sealed up by the Survivalist—"

"Norman W. Nechs," he said.

"Right you are, Sir," I said. "The isotope assay proves that. It was made much later—made in present time, more or less. So it couldn't have been dug up inside the barrel."

Rouse nodded at me. He had a massive head on that round massive body, and it moved slowly, and not much. "Ha," he said. "Unless someone else had come along first, and planted it there. Left it for us to dig up. Assumed no one would ever question a thing, the fools, whoever they were."

I cleared my throat. You can follow me around for years and never hear me do that except when having a cold. I wasn't having a cold just then. "Well, Sir," I said, :"I think the dig crew—the door-openers—would have noticed if there'd been any previous digging up of the site."

"Doormen," Rouse said. "We call them doormen. God alone knows why, but we do. Even the women—some of them are—we call them doormen."

"Yes, Sir," I said. "They'd have noticed, wouldn't they?"

His head moved again. A nod, I think. "Hell, boy, we'd all have noticed. Nobody lives around there—where we dug. Nobody's lived around there for a hundred years. We found animal markings—paws, claws, that sort of thing. We expect that. A lot of drift, tumble, anything that can happen to dirt and rock left alone a while. Digging would have left signs. We'd have seen those, and they weren't there."

"Then nobody could have planted the manuscript inside that barrel?" I said.

"Oh, Hell, I suppose not," he said. "Someone switched it for the real thing later on. During transport to the library. While it was sitting around *waiting* for transport. Something like that—had to be something like that, boy."

"Knave," I said. "Gerald Knave. And—what could it have been switched for? There *is* no Heinlein manuscript of *The Stone Pillow*. Heinlein said there wasn't."

"How the Hell should I know?" he said. His head waggled. "He was some nut. He wrote science-fiction. He might have said anything." He snorted. "Good Lord, boy, how else could the thing have happened? It had to be that way."

I shook my own head. "It didn't," I said. "There was no other manuscript called *The Stone Pillow* to substitute for it. The thing had to be put in place between the time the barrel was dug up, and the time the manuscript was seen by–well, Sir, by more than the dig crew."

Rouse snorted again. "That," he said, "is impossible. You're telling me that one of the techs opening the barrel slipped this forgery into it. Why, none of them would have the knowledge or the resources to commit a forgery that would cozen a six-year-old child."

"Perhaps not," I said. "I don't know them. But one of them might have been paid to do the job. Or–well, one of the dig crew might have done it. You were all there, all very quickly after the barrel was opened–"

"Of course we were, boy," he said. "We had an interest in it. You can understand that. Anyone can understand that."

I tried once more. "Knave, Sir," I said, feeling more and more like the schoolboy I had once been, very long ago. "Gerald Knave. It's my name, Sir."

He stared at me. "Damn it," he said, "I know it's your name, boy." I sighed and gave up, more or less silently. "But what you're telling me is impossible. I know those people. To think that one of them would do such a thing–I tell you, there has to be another explanation."

I shrugged. "The trouble is," I said, "there really isn't. How many techs were there doing the job of opening that thing?"

"Three," he said instantly. "It usually is–nothing terribly demanding about that job, nothing to require an expanded crew. They've done that sort of work before, many times before. All but Machias, of course–he was new then. I think it was his first assignment after training."

I had an interesting thought, and didn't let it show on my face. Instead I asked for the names of the techs, and where they could now be found. Rouse gave me the names at once, then fished around on his desk, pushing paper piles here and there, and pulled out a sheet of printed fax paper.

"Assignments list," he said. He read off current job assignments for the three people, told me where the jobs would have them located, and said: "Well, boy? Anything else?"

I had six hundred questions, and asked none of them. "If I need to come back, Sir, I'll inquire first, of course."

Another snort. "You damn well will," he said. "And make an appointment, and keep it. I'm a busy man, boy. Busy." He waved a hand at the piles of papers.

"I can see that, Sir," I said, "and thanks for your time."

It took me fifteen minutes, once I was out of there, to return to my normal age and weight.

TWENTY-NINE

I SPENT THE rest of the afternoon talking to techs, bothering them at their work—and getting very little worth the bother, damn it. I see no reason to report on the conversations I had with Filomene Hass or Roget de Lisle—I might mention de Lisle's pride in what he was dead sure was ancient-French ancestry, and may have been for all I knew; God knows I am not an expert on the splinter cultures of preSpace Earth—but nothing in either talk was of any use, and very little of it was of any interest to speak of.

Drang Mathias, on the other hand, deserves a little mention. In his own way, he was as colorful a character as Gro Rouse had been.

"I'm not going to be stuck in this dead-end job forever," he told me, pugnaciously. He was a pugnacious type, a medium-tall man with a lumpy build and exceptionally broad shoulders. We were sitting in one of the lab rooms—either the one in which Norman W. Nechs' barrel had been opened, or a reasonable facsimile—and Drang Mathias was doing about as much sitting as two or three average people. He was sprawled over a lightweight plastic chair, with his feet up on another one, and one arm cocked casually behind him on a bare lab table.

"Well, I should hope not," I said. I'd known the man all of twenty seconds.

"I'm going to be a wheel," he said. I stared at him.

"A what?"

"A wheel," he said. "An important person. A mover and a shaker."

Local slang, I thought with some relief; a man announcing he was going to turn into a wheel was not something I ran into every day, and I was just as glad to find out that it wasn't so. (It turns out, by the way—if you care—that it *isn't* local slang. Ravenal had had a craze for late-Twentieth slang eight or nine years before, and some of the terms, like "wheel" and "mover and shaker", had stuck. Apparently on preSpace Earth there were *lots* of people turning into wheels.)

"Good for you," I said. "What I wanted to talk to you about—"

"Head up a department some day," Mathias said. "Disposal, maybe. Not much work, when you're the head of the thing. Everybody else does that. And what's in my way? A couple of exams. A little study, I will go through the exams like—like—"

"Like a wheel," I said, and he nodded.

"Right," he said.

"I'm sure you will," I said. "But it's about an opening you did a few years ago that I wanted to—"

"Opening?" he said. "Dull work, always is. Lots of precautions, but nothing ever happens. Get the thing open, whatever it is, take out the junk, whatever *that* is, sign out your time. Can't even pad a worksheet much—too many other people around."

I made a sympathetic kind of noise. "This particular job," I said, "was a barrel. Inert atmosphere, under slight pressure. The barrel contained some artifacts, and some papers."

"Sounds about right," he said. "We get a lot of that. Sometimes barrels, sometimes boxes or any damn thing."

"Would there be any way of checking back on that one particular job?" I said. "You might remember something about it."

I'd already talked to the two other techs involved, and they'd loaded me with worksheet listings, reports and the like, so I wasn't just blindly guessing about any of this. Mathias sighed, and nodded reluctantly.

"I could go and find the sheets for it," he said. "It's all on record. I'd remember something from the sheets. Is this really important?"

I assured him that a) it was, and b) I had the work sheets right there with me. He sighed again and nodded, and I passed him the sheets, and he read at them for a couple of minutes, making little muttering sounds under his breath. Then he looked up.

"I remember that one," he said. "Naturally I do. That was the one with all the trouble."

I did not smile; it might have interrupted him a little. I said: "Trouble? Tell me about it."

"There was a young one there," he said. "Before we got to open the thing. One of the dig crew. Not a real babe, you know—" I recognized another bit of late-Twentieth slang—"but not just cold oatmeal, either. You had nothing better to do, she would be a fair jump, you know?"

"Before you opened the thing," I said. Not interrupting him, just gently pushing him along.

Maybe, just maybe, this was something.

"She was all kinds of worried," Mathias said. "Said this was a special job, very important. What she wanted was to be there during the opening."

"And was she?"

Mathias snorted. "Hell of a thing to allow that," he said. "No way in the world. She had to be outside. Precautions, it's all in the book. You catch me going against the book, it will have to be for a babe and a half—I'm not going to be stuck in this dead-end job forever."

"So you said," I told him. Gently, unobtrusively. Non-interruptedly. "And she didn't get to be here when you opened the barrel?"

"None of them did," Mathias said. "But he was there, like five seconds after the thing was open and the warning light went off—automatic, you know."

I said: "He?"

"She wasn't there for maybe five minutes," Mathias said. "With the other ones on the dig crew. Five, ten minutes, everybody was there. But he was there right away—I figure he had seniority, he was making sure everything was done right. She must have told him he couldn't get in during, but right after was fine—which is what I'd told her. She argued like Hell over it, but she took it."

"He?" I said. "Who he?"

The answer seemed to take several years in coming. When it did come I had the feeling that pieces clicked together inside my head. Not all of them, not even most of them. But, at last, one piece seemed to fit some other pieces.

"The old guy," Mathias said. "Mouse. Something like Mouse."

"Rouse," I said. "Grosvenor Rouse."

Mathias nodded. "You got it," he said.

THIRTY

I'D SCHEDULED PAULA SHORE—the young one, the more-or-less satisfactory babe—for the next morning. I wanted very badly to change the appointment, and rush up to see her within the next thirty seconds.

I did nothing of the kind. A piece had clicked in—and before I knew what I wanted to ask Paula Shore—or Grosvenor Rouse, for that matter—I was going to have to sit down and do some hard thinking.

I was also going to have to consult with Master Higsbee. And just possibly—at second hand, I was sure—with little Robbin Tress. When I did get back to the apartment—and I took my time over it, and went out to dinner, though not to the Art Café; I was slowing myself down and giving the back of my head a little time to work, but I don't think I could have taken another conversation just then with Corri Reges and Chandes Washington, on any subject under the local sun—when I did get back, I found a message waiting for me.

Old Forgetful at work, damn it: I had neglected to instruct the damned thing, and my pocket piece had, naturally, been as silent as the grave of (choice of one or both) Ramsay Leake or Norman W. Nechs.

And I was going to hear about it, too—because the message was from Master Higsbee.

"Gerald, there has been rather an odd development," his rasp told me. "Please meet me, and Robbin, as soon as you get this message." He told me where, and I gave a small but powerful curse. "Her therapists think it a good idea, and I have, of course, acceded to their wishes in the matter, as it can make no real difference to you."

Little did he know the difference it made to me, and I was not about to tell him. The message was twenty-eight minutes old when I heard it. God damn it, it had taken me thirty-five to forty minutes to get to the apartment from the place at which I had so slowly and casually dined.

Well, it would take me less time than that getting back to the damned

Art Café to meet the two of them—if I had to bribe a local cabbie with all the treasures of Ravenal, and steal Geraint Beauthis' half-ream of antique paper to add in.

* * *

IT TURNED OUT that I wasn't meeting the two of them after all; I was meeting the three of them. The Master and Robbin were sharing a back corner booth in the place—there were a few booths, though most of the place was old-fashioned open tables—with another old friend, B'russ'r B'dige.

Shock upon shock, so to speak—Robbin actually out in public in a restaurant—and B'russ'r himself in the place. That little Robbin was comfortable around B'russ'r was no great surprise; Berigot were people she'd been able to accept for some years. They had, as far as Robbin was concerned, few emotions, and therefore posed no threat to speak of.

Whether her talents extended to them—whether (for instance) her feeling that the ringleader (or associate ringleader) of the damned forgery and theft was someone I'd met included Berigot as well as humans—I wasn't at all sure. Nobody knew how the talent worked, and that particular question—were Berigot included in the futures she saw—had never quite come up.

Best to assume it did, and they were, of course.

But seeing her out in a public restaurant—even in a rather dim and secluded back booth—was like seeing her in the middle of a Year Day parade back on Earth, waving grandly from a float depicting the Incorporation of Grand Forks, Iowa. It took me a few seconds to get my breath back, and smile, and greet everybody.

B'russ'r inclined his head to the right; I gave mine a nod to the left. Little Robbin gave me a small, slightly nervous smile.

"Hello there, Sir," she said in that breathless little voice. "I'm so glad to see you, Master Higsbee was *sure* you'd make it here but I was *worried*, there's so much traffic out on the streets, you know, it's hard to be sure of anything."

The streets had been as crowded as they get on Ravenal—or in City Two, at any rate; traffic in City One, where the bureaucracy mostly works, does crowd up on you at times—which is not very. "It isn't so bad, once you get used to it," I said. "I'm sure you will, too. It's wonderful to see you out like this."

"Oh, I'm doing all kinds of things, Sir," she said. "I went to First Files

Building to meet B'russ'r here, I really did, and went through the doors and the turnstile and everything."

"Wonderful," I said, and meant it. The Master was fixing me with a glittering eye. Not a pleasant eye.

"Gerald," he said, "it is very kind of you to accept the invitation of an old, blind man. It has been one hour since my call to you, an hour forever lost in the past, an hour that might perhaps have been used."

Oh, God. "I forgot the damned pager again," I said. "Sorry."

The eye glittered just a hair more. "Tell me, Gerald," he said quietly. "When you left to meet us here, did you remember to instruct your apparatus?"

I smiled at him. Maybe he could feel the smile somehow. "I did, Sir," I said.

He gave me a curt nod. Perhaps a shade disappointed. "Good," he said.

"Now," I said, and sat down. The Master had been having the eggplant parmigiana. Robbin had some sort of salad, or what looked like the remains of a salad. There were three empty glasses in front of her, and a fourth one half-full of what looked like, and certainly was, a chocolate milkshake. B'russ'r—who wasn't sitting, of course, but leaning casually against a side wall of the booth—had been drinking something bright red from a closed bottle, like a no-G squeeze affair. Specially ordered in, I supposed, for a distinguished guest.

I gave them all a smile. "What's new?"

"Oh, it's about the shooting," Robbin said. "Of the birds, you know. When the three birds were hurt, long long ago."

B'russ'r never so much as turned a hair, though Berigot a) are not birds, nor avian in any way, and b) rather dislike being taken for such things.

"In fact," the Master rasped at me, "it was the police who turned the fact up. They very kindly shared it with B'russ'r, and he has shared it with us, and now with you."

I took a deep breath. The puzzle-piece I'd found was connected to the manuscript, and that end of things. If something had now turned up about the Berigot shootings five years before, perhaps it would connect with my new piece.

Perhaps the whole puzzle was beginning to take on a recognizable shape, I told myself. Hope (as a writer named Dickerson, either Gordon or Emily, said preSpace) is the thing with feathers, not to be confused with B'russ'r B'dige.

Not to be confused with the facts of the real universe, either. "It seems the three Berigot–" the Master began.

And B'russ'r did something I had never seen a human being do–Robbin Tress excepted. He interrupted the Master. "G'ril Mnus," he said, "G'mancae B'dint, and B'dyr G'ridget."

Master Higsbee nodded at him–not at him, in his general direction. Being a Blind Man, who couldn't quite locate the speaker. It underlined massive irritation; but none of it showed in his voice.

"Exactly," he said. "G'ril and G'mancae and B'dyr had, it now seems, an acquaintance in common."

My eyebrows went up. Maybe the Master felt the air motion. "Of course they did," I said. "Most Berigot know each other, after all. The way most humans in an outpost on a non-human planet know each other. It goes with the territory."

"No," Master Higsbee said, and gave a small, savage smile. "A human acquaintance in common. The police had thought nothing of it, since he was only an acquaintance, though fairly close to two of the three; they could find no connection between him and any of the shootings. I am advised–assured–that they are now–ah–rethinking."

If the human acquaintance was who I thought it might be, I told myself, all sorts of pieces were going to click into place.

But it wasn't. I said: "All right, that's different. And, I agree, very greatly interesting. Who?" And the Master said:

"Ramsay Leake."

THIRTY-ONE

AFTER A LONG, long second, I said: "Well."

After about four more seconds I said: "But all this establishes is that Leake was connected to the whole thing. And we knew that already."

"You've missed rather an interesting point," the Master said. He threw it away, casually—which is worse than underlining the fact that Gerald Knave had been being stupid. I tried not grinding my teeth, and put on an attentive expression. Who knew what he was capable of noticing? Any normal person would have had his eyes restored thirty years before.

He was waiting for his acknowledgment, and I gave it to him. "I might have," I said. Mildly. "Go ahead."

"There are two roads to this conclusion," the Master said. Robbin was working away at her salad, or whatever it was—it had fruits in it, and nuts, and tomatoes, and a lot of things I was too occupied to identify, all covered in a white, lumpy goo—and B'russ'r was leaning patiently, listening. "The first you may have been too hurried by events to notice. The second has just come to our attention." He paused, took a fork, and twirled spaghetti onto it, guiding himself just a bit with his left hand. He handles spaghetti very well. "The connection has been underlined by the—ah—acquaintanceship," he said. "And it goes back further than five years, in two cases—and just over five years, in the third case."

"So Ramsay Leake met one of the Berigot just around the time of the shootings," I said. "What does this tell us?"

"It tells us—since we know that a connection between Leake and the shootings must exist—that the meeting was purposeful." The Master twirled a little more spaghetti. B'russ'r sucked on his bright red thing and nodded, shifting slightly against the wall.

"Then Leake was actively involved," I said.

"Oh, yes," the Master said. "But that isn't the main point, Gerald. The main point is that the entire plan regarding the forged Heinlein manuscript has been in existence for at least five years."

B'russ'r nodded again. Robbin took a forkful of tomatoes, nuts and goo. I said, very slowly: "For at least a year before anybody dug up Norman W. Nechs and his little hoard."

"At least that, yes."

I was hurried, I suppose. I said a stupid thing. "Then someone, somewhere, knew about Nechs, and knew he was a Heinlein collector, and–"

The Master stopped me with a kindly wave of his hand, which was full of fork and spaghetti. "Gerald," he said very mildly, "you must control this tendency of yours to–ah–rush off in all directions. That is simply not the case; it could not be so, and therefore it is not so."

"But–" I said, and then stopped the mad rush, and thought, and said: "Oh."

"Precisely," the Master said. "A target–"

"Of opportunity," B'russ'r said. "The plan waited for the discovery of a suitable hoard, somewhere on Earth. Once that discovery had been made, and was known, it could be put into practice quickly. The forged manuscript would have been ready and waiting for opportunity."

A consequence of information upload, of course–and I had uploaded that much of it myself, once I'd taken thought just a little–but he really should have known better. He knew *something* about Master Higsbee, after all, and he might have seen that the Master was not fond of interruptions.

The Master looked in his general direction again–not at him, just vaguely out there somewhere. The Blind, Helpless Stare, perhaps a little overdone to my taste. He gestured with his loaded fork–and carelessly let it fall while his hand was in motion. The fork landed at the far edge of the table, splattering bits of spaghetti and sauce here and there, and falling short of B'russ'r himself by about four inches. If I'd asked the Master–at the time, or at any moment of his life from then on–he'd have given me the miss distance in microns.

"Oh my," he said. "I am sorry, Sir. Would you mind–ah–retrieving it for me? I'm blind, you know."

B'russ'r moved a step or two to the side, to give himself room, and picked the fork up in one small hand. He leaned forward across the table, his left wing narrowly missing Robbin's plate of things and goo, and put the fork on Master Higsbee's plate, carefully making a sound with it, plinking the fork handle on the edge of the plate. "There you are, Master," he said. His voice was even and respectful. What else could it have been? "It is just to your right, on the plate."

"Thank you," Master Higsbee said. "I am most grateful. It is a terrible thing, to be blind."

"It must be," B'russ'r said. "To lose an entire sense. But surely there is medical aid, Master. I have heard that you will not accept it, but—"

"It cannot be done," the Master said, an outright lie, or else a statement that the Master's rules *were* the rules of the universe. He reached for the fork, without hesitation or a wrong move, and smiled. "Thank you for your concern, Sir."

"Just so," B'russ'r said, and the moment passed off. I was some relieved, myself; I'd thought there might have been bloodshed. But Master Higsbee had made his move, received an apology—and managed to interrupt B'russ'r, just to even matters up.

Robbin had never paused in stoking her own little furnace, but she paused now. "What could it be that's so interesting about the time, Sir?" she said. "I mean, whoever did all this had to have time to get everything ready, didn't he? Or she or whatever. To make the paper and get the story written, whatever it is, and just get everything ready. Isn't that obvious?"

"Of course it is, dear child," the Master said. "But what we now know is that the plan was in full operation as long as a year before the dig. Leake could not have been the principal player—in fact, his task in all of this is comparatively simple to deduce, I should think. Gerald?"

I'd been waiting for that, and was ready, thank God; I had had enough of looking stupid in front of bright people. "Leake was a computer expert," I said. "And there's really only one spot for a computer expert in all of this, as we all assumed from the start—making the analogues of isotope patterns, so that the paper could be prepared."

"Well," the Master said slowly, "there is another possibility, Gerald. There is such a thing as computer analysis of style; he might have been called upon to analyze the Heinlein style for the actual writing itself." He sighed, cut and took in some eggplant parmigiana without any noticeable Blind Man antics, and admitted: "But it is of such low probability, it can effectively be ignored. In any case, computer analysis of style has never given any solidly dependable result."

"So I thought," I said. "That's why I didn't mention it."

"No," he went right on, ignoring me, "Leake would have taken the isotope patterns from a sheet of contemporary paper—easily enough available even today, though fax paper is far more common—and had it 'run back' by computer through time, so to speak, to the putative date of the manuscript. Then he would have performed a second computer operation, constructing an isotope pattern suitable for material from the mid-Twentieth century, surviving until the present. All in all, not a terribly complex job for anyone at ease with that sort of programming—as many variables as isotopes, each with its own half-life and rate of change."

"And when he had it nicely back into the year he'd picked, and then forward again to present time," I said, "that was the recipe for the faked twentieth-century paper."

"Clearly so," the Master said. "The question is, of course: for whom was he doing this small job? And who was it who apparently grew afraid that he might weaken and speak to someone, and so has paid him so—very finally for doing it?"

"There is another question," B'russ'r said. "Given the recipe, how in fact was the paper made? There exists no instrumentality capable of creating such a paper, to that degree of detail."

"Whatever the instrumentality is," the Master said, "it is clearly new—someone has invented something—and it is, as clearly, imperfect. Some of the isotopes were not correct for the purported dating of the paper."

"I am given to wonder," B'russ'r said. "Could the invention itself have led to the idea of the forgery? Having hit upon such a technique, would this person then have thought to use it in such a manner?"

Fencing was still going on, I noticed. "Unimportant," the Master said casually. "If he thought of the forgery first, and then invented a method of accomplishing his task almost—though not quite—perfectly, or if he came upon the method, and then bethought himself of forgery as a profitable use—what difference can it make?"

B'russ'r rustled his wings. Small objection. "Any small fact about this person," he said, "may serve to identify him. If we know his psychology, for instance—"

The Master gave his bark of a laugh. "You have allowed the twentieth century to infect you, B'russ'r," he said. "Even today, Psychological Statics is not a science in the true sense. In those days, there were fools who believed that it was."

I put in: "They didn't call is Psychological Statics."

I was annihilated without effort. "They had a number of names for the thing," the Master said. "They never did call it by its proper name–which was, in that era, Nonsense." He turned back to B'russ'r–no foolery now about getting a vague fix on him, but a direct glittering stare. "This miscreant will be found," he said, "through his traces. He has left many, and it only remains to interpret them properly. His psychology is his own affair, and I wish him well of it."

B'russ'r ducked his head a bit and spread his little hands. A shrug of sorts. "It may be so."

Round one to the Master.

THIRTY-TWO

THE FACT–THAT Leake had known all three of the wounded Berigot, and had met the latest one just before the shootings began–got discussed thoroughly. There were implications on implications, and between the four of us we built and demolished several large sand castles of theory. Robbin, who put in a word here and there, mostly questions, came up with the wildest one of the night: an unknown alien race that had planted the forgery because it contained statements that would slowly addle the minds of all human beings who encountered it.

I didn't consider that one for more than a minute and a half, myself, and I think I spent seventy or eighty seconds longer on it than either B'russ'r or the Master did. It was certainly a showy idea, and it had its attractions for me on that ground if no other–but an alien race that had set out to addle the collective mind of humanity by planting one (1) manuscript by one (1) writer three full centuries old and more in one (1) library on one (1) planet seemed just a tad implausible. As advertising people have been finding out for more centuries than Heinlein's *real* work has been around, there are far better and simpler ways to addle human minds.

But there were other notions–the first and best being the Master's statement, early in our talk, that all the files belonging to Ramsay Leake, going back at least six years–a year before anything had begun–should get the most careful examination possible, and then some.

"It will be a daunting prospect," B'russ'r said. "I agree that it should be done, if at all possible–but six years of computer files, for a computer expert like Mr. Leake, will represent many hours of work, even if codes can be had."

"And," I said, "if anything turns up I will, personally, be surprised as Hell."

"I see both your points," Master Higsbee said. "But no matter how we are daunted, we must proceed–and, though he has had years of time in which to destroy such files, and will know far better than most how to accomplish such destruction tracelessly and completely, we can hope that he slipped somewhere. Such things happen, and very often."

"They do indeed," I said. "It has to be done. But it's the Hell of a job of work, for what I will bet is no return."

But of course it didn't have to be done. Robbin looked up dreamily from her fruits, tomatoes and goo. She took rather a noisy suck at the straw sticking out of her latest milkshake, and said: "He didn't forget anything much. There's a dated memo five years old somewhere, but it's blank. That's all there is, sorry."

Days, possibly weeks, of work accomplished for us in one eyeblink. Nobody thought of doubting Robbin, though I wondered privately just how such information got to her. It seemed to me there were two possibilities:

1) Somehow, her wild talent had examined all the files, wherever the Hell they were and however encoded, while we sat there discussing them. This argued that her talent had more speed to it than computers did, not to mention an awesome gift for cracking codes.

2) Her wild talent had looked into the future, after we'd done all the hard work of examining the damned files, and told us what we'd have found when the job was done. This led to considerations that boggled my mind just a trifle: if we now took her word for the results, as we were doing, and *didn't* go through the files, as we certainly *weren't* going to do—what became of her picture of the future? In the real future, we wouldn't have looked at the files at all—so how had she seen a future in which we had?

"There are answers, of course, and answers for the answers; there always are." A science-fiction writer, preSpace (not Heinlein, and I am damned if I can put a name to him or her), had written that line, and I'd treasured it for years. There were answers to the questions posed by either explanation of little Robbin's talent. That the answers led to more, and hairier, questions was of course expectable, this being the kind of universe it is.

And none of the answers, and none of the resulting questions, have a damned thing to do with Ramsay Leake, or three wounded Berigot, or a manuscript that hadn't, in fact, belonged to Norman W. Nechs. It's a fascinating field of study—and there are people on Ravenal to this day studying away at it—but it belongs in some other report. The results of her talent, as described, did, and do, belong in this one.

We agreed Leake's files didn't have to be combed through—not by us. Detective-Major Gross could do the job, and we wished him joy of it, but we could go right on to something else.

The question was, of course: What else? and there wasn't much disagreement. B'russ'r and Master Higsbee were handed the tough job, and the thankless one—combing for any link between Leake and anyone at all involved with the dig, with the unsealing of the damned barrel, or with the manuscript. Master Higsbee volunteered the information—I had no idea where he'd got it, or when, but I'd as soon question a Ravenal datafile—that Leake had not been a reader of science-fiction, and had thought it, he'd once told somebody or other, "amusingly primitive". But whether he knew some of the Ravenal Misfits in other connections we couldn't be sure, and the combing would start at once, for them and for anyone else even remotely in the picture.

The job was tough, just because it had so many damn details about it. And it was thankless, because the chances were very large that no connection that meant anything was going to be found; whoever was behind all this had been careful right through, as far as we could tell, and there was no reason for him, her or them to show a streak of carelessness as regarded Leake. The man was, after all, dead, which argued that somebody wanted secrecy preserved, and was willing to extend himself a little to ensure it.

But it had to be done—and this time Robbin didn't have one of her helpful little visions. We were stuck with actually doing it.

I, on the other had, was going to go right on talking to people. Paula Shore first, and then Freda Hocksher. And somewhere in there, another talk with Grosvenor Rouse, to which I did not look forward.

And some of the Misfits as well—Mac, for one, and probably Corri Reges and Chandes Washington and Bitsy Bowyer for three more. I had some more facts now, which led to sixty or seventy new questions to ask.

All in all, a busy day coming up. With Paula Shore right at the start of it. A babe, I had been told, if not quite a completely satisfactory babe.

I spent the evening thinking up questions to ask a babe, and crafting several fine approaches to a variety of subjects involving manuscripts, digs and science-fiction. I managed to persuade myself to get some sleep, and though I can't tell you what dreams I had—when I do remember dreams, they're too silly ever to repeat—I must have had some, because I woke myself up, somewhere around 3 A. M., shouting: "Where are Heinlein's isotopes?"

It was not a question I could answer, so I went back to sleep.

THIRTY-THREE

Paula Shore's office was as different from Gro Rouse's as two offices could be. It did have a desk in it, and a computer-reader, some casual impedimenta, and three chairs. The casual impedimenta were six or seven pieces of paper (neatly arranged in a tiny stack), two 3D photos of objects I couldn't identify—out of some dig or other, clearly—lying on the desk, and a large stone mug filled with tea, also on the desk and convenient to Paula Shore's left hand. It had two people in it, Paula Shore and Yours Very Truly.

It had nothing else in it at all. The place was picked as clean as a bone; personal objects, clutter of any sort, were more conspicuous by their absence than anything whatever had been in Gro Rouse's crowded room full of knick-knacks and Rouse. The word I'm groping for is "sterile", and when I saw the place, and saw Paula Shore, it was clear to me at once why Drang Mathias hadn't called her a *real* babe. There was nothing at all wrong with her—au contraire, as they say; she was a little woman of about 27, but her figure was lovely, her face elfin and earnest (which is a fetching combination) behind very large, horn-rimmed glasses so old-fashioned they were charming, her hair wavy and raven-black.

And she was very nearly not there at all.

It wasn't anything physical. It was her mood and her manner; she was as thoroughly turned off as if she'd had a little switch on her back frozen in the down position. And while it might have been me—I've had some odd effects on a few people, now and then—I don't really think it was; I think something had frozen that switch for her years before, and she'd simply carried bravely on, going through the motions.

She said: "I understand you wanted to see me, Mr. Knave," and though few people Mr. me—I seem to be just Knave to most of the world, exceptions like little Robbin and the Master (and, God help us, Gro Rouse) duly noted—I didn't even think of correcting her. Whatever the programming was, I was willing to live with it. It was, it seemed to me, programming—not choice.

I told her I did indeed, and it was about the dig she'd been on four years before, with Grosvenor Rouse, and Bitsy Bowyer, and—

"Dean Rell and—oh yes, Freda. I do remember that. There was such a fuss made about the artifacts, you know."

I thought my best approach was—now that, having seen her, I had scrapped all the approaches I'd had saved up for her—not to mention Drang Mathias and his story at all, until and unless I had to. So I said, blandly: "Fuss?"

"Dr. Rouse was very particular about them," she said. "He wanted to be there when the container was breached. Of course I knew that wasn't usual practice—not at all, one never is, it's left to the technicians entirely—but he thought an exception might be made. He wanted me to ask to be present."

Well, it was like getting information from a computer, with the slight difference that this computer was perfectly capable of deciding to lie to you. I mean, without your having programmed that sort of antic into it first. Punch in a question, and an answer popped out. I remembered a planet I'd been on once, where the clean-room superstition about computers—no dust allowed, and damn little breathing—had taken firm hold, and made life inconvenient for everybody. Paula Shore's bare office gave me an echo of it.

"Dr. Rouse wanted to be there," I said. "So he asked you to ask to be present. That sounds just a little odd."

"He felt he didn't want to—'swing his weight around' in the labs," she said. You could hear the inverted commas dropping around the slang phrase. "If I were permitted to be present, then Dr. Rouse would be as well; that seemed obvious. But I am much younger in the field than Dr. Rouse, and so have much less influence. He determined that it would be better that I ask for the exception. It was not, in any case, granted."

"But you didn't particularly want to be there," I said.

"I had no reason to be there," she said. "My job had been done. There was some curiosity about the contents of the artifact—a large container of some sort, though I don't recall exactly what—"

"A barrel," I said. "Under slight pressure, and containing manuscript, and some metal object."

She gave me a nod. It wasn't at all the brisk, robotic nod I expected, but a perfectly human movement of her head. "Thank you; was it really?" she said. "In any case, there was some curiosity–but scarcely enough to wish to breach normal practice."

"But Dr. Rouse felt something more.:"

"I imagine he must have," she said. "I should think Dr. Rouse would be the one to ask about that, Mr. Knave."

"You don't have any idea what it might have been?"

"The metal, perhaps,." she said. "Dr. Rouse is something of a–collector." I had the feeling she'd substituted the word for a more acid one at the last second, possibly Bitsy Bowyer's pet, "jackdaw". "He might have wanted to see it, perhaps even to bargain for custodianship of it; he apparently enjoys displaying such things."

I remembered Rouse's cluttered office, with the few artifacts I thought I could place, from Alphacent, and the many apparently from Earth. "He does have a good many items in his office," I said.

"He has said he–gets something from seeing them, touching them. A species of knowledge; he has called it that." She shrugged; a little abrupt, but still quite a human shrug. "It may be something of the sort. But he also enjoys the display."

"Well," I said, "some people do. Collectors–people who just enjoy old things. Special things. Souvenirs." I was babbling, and not quite realizing it–not at that second. I was sitting in that bare office, looking at Paula Shore, and listening to her, in a way.

But I was also in several other places, all at once. Pieces were connecting all over my head, and I was getting ideas.

Right at that moment, I had no damned idea what the ideas were. I seldom do, at that point; I only know I have them, and when I get a little time and room I can sit down and look for them, and take them to wherever in my head I can manage to clear a little space, so I can get them all nicely identified, classified and sorted.

Paula Shore had said something–about the barrel, about Gro Rouse, about artifacts in general or digs in general; sooner or later I'd know just what–and the something had echoed something else I'd heard, and thought about—and had set pieces connecting all over. I knew who had managed the forgery, headed up the theft, shot at three Berigot—and killed Ramsay Leake.

I knew how it had all been done—well, in that area there were still some sizable holes, but they were holes I thought I could fill, given some time for thinking, and some hard thinking.

I even thought I knew *why* it had all been done—which was (I felt) the most unusual part of the whole business.

All I needed—I told myself, while Paula Shore said something about the drive for collecting things being a relic of our remote simian ancestry, somehow or other—was a little time, and I would know what it was I knew.

Just at that moment, all I knew was, I knew it.

No—I knew one more thing. I knew the core of the whole thing—the single fact that lit up all the other facts.

The core was: Nothing made any sense whatever.

THIRTY-FOUR

WELL, IT WAS really too much to hope for. When I left Paula Shore's office, I found a vacant spot, pulled out my pocket piece, and punched in the code for Master Higsbee.

If he'd neglected to instruct his machine to forward to his pocket piece—well, as I say, it was really too much to hope for. The Master, God damn it, doesn't do things like that. I would pay six times the fee Ping Boom was paying me, just offhand, if he only would, just once, and I could know about it.

But the phone beeped twice, telling me it was forwarding, and then blipped once. It was in mid-second-blip when the Master's rasp said: "Who?"

"Gerald Knave," I said. "We must talk." And as I said it, I began to know what the Hell it was we'd be talking about. The things I knew started to filter through to me, and I discovered what they were. It had taken days to get to the point at which I knew something—but only minutes, thank God, to get from there to actually finding out what it was I knew.

He was patient. "Gerald, I am assorting a great many data. Can conversation wait until there is time available?"

"I'm starting to see just what the data is going to attach itself to," I said. "That may help your assorting job."

"Do you mean—ah—that you begin to see daylight?"

The Master sounded amused. I wasn't at all sure why. "It's more like seeing—oh, three o'clock in the morning," I said. "I wouldn't call it daylight. But I do see something. And this is no place to talk about it—I'm in some sort of waiting-room for a set of offices. I've been talking to Paula Shore."

"Three o'clock in the morning," he said. "If that is so—if you have seen some of the darkness—then I am pleased, Gerald. And I agree that we should talk, if only to ensure that you are seeing the correct darkness. Go home. Call from there. You will have privacy and ease—and I will be enabled to continue my work with minimal interruption."

"Well—" I said.

"Finished," he said.

Click.

So I went on home.

* * *

I SETTLED IN, made a pot of Sumatra Mandheling, drank the first half-cup, arranged pot, cup, sugar and cream on a low shelf near the phone, lit an Inoson cigarette—why not give the Master all the time available to get on with his assorting?—and punched in the number. As I heard the two forwarding beeps I remembered, cursed under my breath and put out the damn cigarette.

"Who?" he said, a second or so later, and I said:

"Me again."

"Ah," he said. "The darkness. Yes. You have begun to see reason behind the forgery, and the theft."

I hesitated a second, and took in a little more coffee. "I wouldn't exactly call it reason," I said.

"Then you *are* beginning to see," he said. "I am pleased, Gerald. It has been only a few days, in all; you have indeed developed."

I swallowed. Hard. "You know something," I said.

"I know a good deal," the unoiled camshaft told me. "You also know something, Gerald. Tell me why the forgery was created, and why the counterfeit Heinlein manuscript was stolen."

Could he be bluffing? I thought. Could it be that he had no idea, was waiting for me to lay it out for him, and would then say calmly that he'd known all along?

No, damn it. But I tested the idea anyhow; I gave him an answer that would make sense only if he *did* know. "Because it was there," I said.

"Exactly, Gerald. Because it was there—in at least two senses."

All right, he knew. And why not? He was, after all, Master Higsbee, who knew everything that could possibly be known. I took in more coffee, looked at the pack of Smoking Tubes lying on the shelf, decided that lighting one would only display childish rancor, and said: "To begin with, because the technique, whatever it was, was available."

"Available to the forger," he said. "Which argues a base of knowledge—though not necessarily his own knowledge."

"In other words, either our forger had the technical facility to cobble up such an assortment of isotopes—or he knew someone who did."

"Have you a preference, Gerald?" he said.

I nodded into the phone. "Of course I do," I said. "He knew someone. If Robbin is right, and I've met the person responsible, it can't be a physicist with a specialty in isotopes—the only one I know, and I've done lists of people I know on Ravenal, is Mac. And I will not believe it of Mac. He'd have done a better job, or no job at all."

"He is not a specialist in that particular small corner of his field," Master Higsbee said. "But I agree he might be able to do the job—and further agree that, if he had, it would have been done more capably." He paused, and gave me a small chuckle. "But you have forgotten one person who might manage the task, Gerald."

"I have?" More coffee. One more glance at the cigarettes. "Who?"

"Myself," the rasp said. "Though old and blind and almost helpless, Gerald, I believe I could, with some thought, manage such a task. It requires no advance in physical theory, but merely refinements of existing methods; it would be difficult and demanding, but quite possible. It is an invention—but not, Gerald, an invention beyond capability."

Oh, God. "Well," I said, "you didn't."

"I will not spoof you, Gerald," he said. "I did not. If I had, once again, I believe the forgery would have been more capably managed."

"Agreed," I said. "And if you didn't do it, and Mac didn't do it, then whoever did this thing—"

"Led the small group which did these things," the rasp corrected me.

More coffee. I'd finished the second cup, and poured myself a third. "Just so," I said.

"Gerald," he said, "you are drinking too much coffee today. You will suffer for it in your nerves."

All right. He'd heard the stuff being poured, and stirred after I'd put in the cream and sugar. Did coffee make a different set of sounds from tea? Or had he simply deduced that, before noon, I wouldn't be drinking tea?

I sighed. "The leader of the pack, then," I said, and heard that dry chuckle again at the Classical allusion, "had to know a specialist."

"Not difficult, on Ravenal, if you are yourself a scholar in virtually any field of science," he said. "There are many such acquaintances; it is not true here that molar physicists, for example, consort only with other molar physicists."

"He heard about the technique, then—heard it was possible, that someone could do such a job and was thinking of doing it—and made the someone a proposition."

"Fame and fortune," the Master said. "But how fortune, for a manuscript that was certain to be given to the Scholarte, that was certain to reside in First Files Building, all unpaid for?"

"How fame, for that matter," I said, "if the forgery were to be undetected?"

"Exactly," the Master said.

I said: "It makes no sense."

"We might enunciate a rule," the Master said.

"We might?" More coffee.

"If it doesn't make any sense,." he said, *"it doesn't make any sense."*

I said it that time. "Ah."

"Which brings us to the second application of your statement: because it was there. First, because the isotope technique was there. Second—because the plan was there."

"But there was no plan," I said. "Not in the sense we've been discussing, since we started."

He said, quietly: "Ah, Gerald, stop and think. Of course there was a plan. But most of it has not yet come to fruition."

"Right," I said. "I was thinking of what *has* happened—not what was going to."

"And now certainly will not," he said, "as we are armed against it."

"The shootings," I said suddenly. "The Berigot. Five years ago."

"And yourself, more recently," he added. "We must put Mr. Leake in another category; that shooting was meant to kill, and did so. Though perhaps—well, never mind it just now, Gerald."

"All right, but we'll get to it, we'll have to, whatever it is," I said. "Master—how much do you know? Have you been carting the whole answer around with you., waiting for somebody else to find it before you said anything?"

The chuckle again. And a fourth cup of coffee. "I have not," he said. "I should feel myself criminally responsible, were that the case. I have seen this much for some time—but not more. The identity of the forger and thief—and murderer—is unknown to me. So is the means by which the theft was accomplished. Getting through the grounds is not difficult—"

"No?" I said. "A pulsating field, with a look every twentieth of a second, from three feet below ground to six feet above?"

"Even below ground, let us say four feet below, there exist tunnels—tunnels can be dug, and later perhaps filled in," he said calmly. "But I doubt the necessity for so laborious—and almost certainly traceable—a means. There exists sailplaning."

I stared at the damn phone. "A group of Berigot thieves?" I said. "I refuse to believe it. Everything we know about the Berigot—"

"The Berigot are not thieves," the Master said. "They lack the incentive; their sins are of a different sort." He paused. Maybe he was drinking coffee. Or assorting something. I didn't have the ears to tell. "But human beings can also sailplane; in the presence of a race which can do so without special equipment, one tends to neglect the obvious. Equipment is not difficult to come by, Gerald, nor difficult, if it come to that, to manufacture."

Well, it *was* obvious. Obvious—as a classic science-fiction story has it—as all Hell. "I suppose so," I said. "A band of thieves, sailplaning over the grounds, right to the window—"

"Where they stop," he said. "And somehow come through the window without leaving a trace." He paused. "Gerald, a group of three people, say, sailplaning, might carry a few pounds of equipment. Several pounds, perhaps—imagine each equipped with sailplane wings, holding ropes or having ropes tied to their bodies, the ropes attached to a bag or hammock filled with whatever items were necessary. They would sailplane to the Berigot perch, which is near that window. But what equipment could simply—cancel out wholly unbreakable windows, windows, like all here, which are sealed permanently into place?"

I had the answer. I really did; the Master had handed it to me, right there and then. And I was damned if I'd give it to him. Talk about neglecting the obvious—well, I'd have that piece to shove into place when the rest was ready for it. "The basic question is unanswered," I said. "Who."

"Indeed, Gerald," the Master said. "And I have not the faintest idea who."

THIRTY-FIVE

"WHO" HAD TO WAIT. We needed either more data, or more thought.

But "how" was beginning to be clear. And "why"—

The Master had said it: If it doesn't make any sense, *it doesn't make any sense*. There was no reason to forge a manuscript by Robert Heinlein, if the manuscript were going to go—with no financial profit to anybody—straight to First Files Building, alias Grand Central Library, and sit there in an antique glass case.

There was no reason to steal the damned manuscript, either; it was already known to be a forgery, so the theft couldn't have been to hide that fact or somehow cover it up. And since it *was* a forgery, there would be no chance of finding an eager buyer for it under a counter somewhere. There are always secret collectors—people who buy things they can't show the world, or even their dearest friends, just for the pleasure of owning a piece of somebody's life, even if they have to take that piece out and look at it in secret. A buyer for an authentic Heinlein manuscript would not have been impossible to find—probably two or three of the Ravenal Misfits would leap at the chance, if offered.

But a buyer for a fake Heinlein manuscript didn't exist. So why steal the thing?

Ping Boom had given me most of the answer, long before, and I'd outlined it myself: Education.

If the manuscript had been left lying around, once it was known to be a forgery—it would have offered a large assortment of clues telling any investigator just how the forgery had been managed—how the paper and ink had been so carefully counterfeited. The technique was (according to Master Higsbee, whose word I was willing to take, God knows) difficult, but not impossibly so; somebody could have come up with it, and created the stuff.

And finding out just how the technique worked might very well tell an investigator who had worked it. Specialists in isotope work weren't fantastically rare on Ravenal, but there weren't six hundred of them, either; it's a fairly small splinter of a field. Previous work by one of the members of that splinter group would certainly point the way to the technique, once you saw in detail what the technique was.

So the theft did have a reason: to interfere with the education of investigators. To keep the technique a secret.

It had that reason—and another reason, too.

As the Master had been pointing out, most of the plan hadn't happened yet. The counterfeit Heinlein had been step one. Step two was going to be—a counterfeit Shakespeare? Villon? Dead Sea Scroll?

Something, at any rate. As the bugs were worked out of the isotope technique—and perhaps even if they weren't; let a little time go by, and people would be just as unwilling to spend money on doing a full assay, and the technique as it stood could defeat a limited one, as the counterfeit Heinlein had—anything you could do a fair imitation of could be forged, and accepted as ancient.

And that forgery would, somehow, not get to First Files Building at all. Despite the laws, there would be an unfortunate disappearance somewhere along the road, or a copy passed off on the librarians after examination and testing had been completed. There exist, as I'd just been saying to myself, private collectors, even for objects they can't display at all.

The Master had seen that much. It struck me that somebody else had seen it, too.

Ping Boom, of course.

Which explained both his need to get the manuscript back, and his secrecy about his reasons. He needed to be able to find out how the job had been done—both in order to locate the perpetrator, and to guard against a future counterfeit—and he wanted very badly not to put ideas in anybody's head. Not even mine. He didn't want to mention the specter of a future forgery.

I knew the why of the forgery and the theft—the forgery had been a test run, so to speak, to make sure everything worked even in the imperfect state of the technique. The theft had been to protect the secret of the forgery, with a bigger one in prospect.

And it had had to be a forgery that would get attention. It had to be an important work by an important figure, one still loved and collected and read. If the technique were to be tested, it had to go up against the sort of testing that would be done on that sort of manuscript—because the next job would be that sort of manuscript.

It might even be—why not?—another Heinlein. Given *The Stone Pillow*, why not *The Sound of His Wings*? Why not *Word Edgewise*?

Oh, probably not—the objections that Heinlein couldn't have written *The Stone Pillow*, because he'd said he hadn't, would apply to the others just as well, and the forgers, having tripped over those once, wouldn't want to trip over them again—why make extra difficulties for yourself? Shakespeare would be safer.

But I will admit to a pang of shamefaced regret. The little bit of *The Stone Pillow* I'd seen had whetted my appetite for the rest, and according to those who had read it, from the Master to Mac to (well, with severe reservations) Corri Reges, the thing had read like good Heinlein. I was going to miss the other Heinlein stories, damn it, even if they weren't Heinleins—when there's no real coffee, even instant becomes drinkable.

Well, as Heinlein himself had said, we pilot always into an unknown future. Who knew what might be out there?

Maybe there were some undiscovered Heinleins out there. If not those three stories, then some other story. Maybe an unpublished story or two, somewhere. Maybe that last collection, the one that hasn't survived, is sitting in some Survivalist burrow that hasn't been dug up yet. Who can say?

A man can hope.

THIRTY-SIX

THE BIG QUESTION, of course, still sat there, as unanswerable as ever.

Who?

For that, nobody had even the ghost of an answer. It was clear, more or less, that finding the manuscript and digging into it to see how the isotope trick had been worked would identify our target, or at least identify the part of it that had done the tech job. But finding the damn manuscript was going to be possible only if we could identify our target first—which was nicely circular.

It was weirdly frustrating. There were several people involved—by hypothesis, a planner, a technical wizard, and almost certainly one more at the very least, to help with the theft if nothing else—any one of whom might have been the actual forger, the writer of the thing.

And with at least three people to look for, we were sitting in the middle of nowhere.

Well—it occurred to me that one small piece of this puzzle might benefit from the application of a little police work. Somebody, after all, had shot three Berigot five years ago—and checking alibis for that would be flatly impossible. But the same somebody had shot Ramsay Leake very, very recently; alibis might be checkable.

It's the sort of thing that turns up regularly on 3V, and very seldom anywhere else; in the average killing, either there are no alibis to deal with, or the alibis, when checked out, check out. Once in a long while an alibi is faked—and when that's done with care, it will often pass as fully checked; there are some people, here and there, who are just as bright as some police officers, here and there.

Alibis are not, in short, the first thing anybody grabs at, in an investigation, though if there is a handy bunch of suspects and nothing truly solid that points to just one of them, police will do the work. But we looked to be reduced to grabbing at some.

All right: I went over a list of people I'd met on Ravenal—the suspect pool for the leader of the pack, so to speak, according to little Robbin Tress. I threw some of them out—Robbin herself, and the Master, and B'russ'r (impossible on grounds of motive if nothing else; I would not believe any of the shootings the work of a Beri), Mac (ridiculous on the face of it—and if that hadn't been enough, the person who'd managed the forgery was not going to be the person who'd blown the whistle on the damn thing), Jamie Arthur and my City Two landlord and a few more here and there. I was left with some reconstructive archaeologists, some Misfits and a handful of technicians like Drang Mathias.

Could we find out where all these people had been at the moment Ramsay Leake had been shot? We had that moment pinned down tightly, by Berigot witnesses. And we were looking, it seemed, for a Hell of a marksman—Leake had been drilled at some distance, stone dead with one shot.

Or had he been? The picture of him grabbing at his chest had had me casually assuming he'd been drilled through the heart—which was not necessarily the case. Did it make any difference exactly where the bullet had gone? Not much, perhaps—any bullet that had him pitching over the roof railing would have done the same job. A ten-story fall would cancel Ramsay Leake thoroughly, no matter where he'd been hit. It wasn't worth talking to Gross about, all by itself. But I had a list of suspects, and Gross was the obvious person to head up a nice, large, professional team and check them out. Police will do the work of checking alibis—if they have a list of suspects to start with. I could provide Gross with such a list, though he wasn't going to like the fact that it depended, basically, on Robbin's arcane damn talent.

So I phoned him, found out with no surprise that he'd packed up and gone home for the day long before—I'd been in a brown study for some time, and am giving you only the high points of it; I'd spent hours barely conscious of anything except the inside of my head—and left a message asking him, as politely as I could, to call me.

Then I brewed some coffee, and did some more thinking. I knew how the theft had been accomplished—and I was saving that to show off for the Master, since it led nowhere in particular as regarded other questions. And I did, after all, have one or two indications about at least one member of the pack, and possibly the leader; it seemed unlikely he'd have been comfortable in any other role. I'd had a couple of illuminations—not enough to hang anything on, but enough to think about.

And when I was finished I gave a deep, deep sigh. I was going to have to talk again to one person I really didn't want to talk to again. I'd known it would come up, but that didn't make it any more pleasant.

Well, a job's a job. And there are worse things in any life. Which, while perfectly true, is surprisingly little comfort.

I picked up the phone again. I made two calls, and then a third, in which I got a mech over at First Files Building, and left a message asking for an appointment, at eleven the next morning (I wanted to be rested for this one, if possible) with Grosvenor Rouse.

I thought he'd be able to fit me in—and he was.

THIRTY-SEVEN

HE GAVE ME a greeting almost worthy of the Master, when I knocked on his office door and opened it at eleven sharp.

"Well?"

"Just a few questions," I said. "I want to make sure I've got everything clear." I came in and sat down in the chair opposite him, and looked at his massive figure across the cluttered desk.

"This is taking altogether too much of my time, boy," he said. "I'm a busy man." He gestured at the piles of paper.

"I know," I said mildly, "and I'm grateful for your time." I didn't feel nearly so Schoolboy this time round, but I tried to act as if I did, just to maintain calm. He was used to Schoolboy Knave. "I was wondering about the dig itself. Which one of you actually found the container?"

"The barrel?" he said. "Dr. Bowyer did. I'm sure of it. She called us all over, and we all got a look right there. An exciting moment, boy, in its way."

"It looked the same then as it did when you got it to the lab here?"

He shook his head, forcefully. "It did not," he said. "It would not. We sprayed it, naturally. Protective sealant. My God, boy, don't you know even that much? We spray anything before we remove it—take photos in situ, measure, examine as we can, and then spray before we move it. Always done that way, always."

"I see," I said. "Who did the spraying?"

"That particular barrel?" he said. "Dr. Shore."

"You're certain?"

"Quite certain," he said. I looked around the office, and picked up one of the items on the desk. It was a pair of ancient Ray-Ban sunglasses, with one lens missing, in a glassex case. He barked at me:

"Be careful with that."

"Interesting object," I said. "Where did it come from?"

"Earth, of course."

I nodded. "I see. Was this from the same dig? Or from some previous dig, or a more recent–"

"Not the same dig," he said. "Had that for a good many years now. I don't remember which dig–they're all the same after a while. Fascinating, boy, don't mistake me–there's nothing like going in and seeing it all for the first time in three hundred years–but the details blur together, after a while."

"I can see how they might," I said, and put the case down. I pointed at a cork flute lying on a shelf. "That's from Alphacent, isn't it?"

"It is," he said. "Ritual object. Not very old–Hell, boy, the world's only been settled a hundred and eighty years or so–but this was buried with one of their leaders. Small-town leader type, and the town died out–we were able to go in, get a few things. Not disturb the Ancestors unduly, you know–well, that's a demanding kind of culture they have there."

"I know," I said truthfully. "I've been there."

He looked at me. "Is this just idle chit-chat, boy?" he said. "I've got things to do–"

"No, Sir, it's not idle," I said. "I was admiring your memory. I've noticed it before."

He frowned. "My memory?"

"Yes, Sir," I said. "The way you can just reel off every detail of a dig like that."

"They blur together, boy," he said. "I've told you that. There's nothing wrong with my memory, but when you do a lot of digs, they seem to blur together in your mind. Perfectly natural."

"I'm sure it is," I said. "I've spoken to Dr. Shore, and Dean Rell–Dr. Rell, I suppose–and Dr. Bowyer, and they're all a bit vague about details of the dig. Even about details of the unsealing back here."

"Unsealing's a tech job," he said. "We don't have much to do with it. We like to see the objects as soon as we can, boy, but there's no reason to remember small details. None at all."

I nodded at him. "Perfectly natural. And even on a dig where some object was particularly important to you–those sunglasses, for instance–a lot of the details would naturally blur into the details of other digs. I'm sure that would be true of anybody."

"It would," he said.

"But," I said, "with this one particular dig—the one I've been asking you about—you do remember every detail, sharp and clear. I noticed it last time we talked, Sir. I noticed it even more today—it's so different from the other digs."

There was a little pause. Not a long one, but Rouse was a more practiced blusterer than he was a liar. Nobody's good at every trade. "Well, you asked me about it," he said. "I had a chance to think. To consult my memory."

"You didn't have a chance to think the other day," I said. "But you had no trouble with the details. You even remembered the names of the techs who had unsealed the barrel."

"I looked for the work assignments—"

"No, Sir," I said. "You remembered all three names, at once, and gave them to me. You even remembered that it was Drang Mathias' first assignment—which didn't matter one way or the other, but you had the fact at your fingertips. No hesitation, not even a second or so to think, Sir. You gave me the names when I asked about them."

"I'm sure I—"

"You checked work assignments after that," I said. "To see where they'd be just now. But you checked assignments for names you'd already given me."

Another pause. "I may have," he said. "Memory's an odd thing, boy. Who's to say what odd details will stick in your mind? I happened to remember the technicians, that's all."

"And every other detail of the dig," I said. "Which one of you found the barrel. Even which one of you did the protective spraying—which is certainly the smallest of details. Memory's an odd thing, Sir. Right. I wonder why it acts that way, for you, about this one dig."

He tried for indignation, and missed it. "Boy, what are you implying here?"

"Well, Sir,": I said, "I think I know why you remembered this dig. And I think I know why you wanted to be in the room when the barrel was unsealed."

"In the room? Who told you I wanted to be in the room? That's never done, boy. Never. I was not in the room—ask any of the technicians. Just ask them."

"I did ask them," I said. "I asked Dr. Shore, too, Sir. She told me how you wanted her to ask to be in the room—assuming that, if she'd be allowed, you certainly would as well."

"What does it matter?" he said. "I wasn't there. When the barrel was opened–"

"You were standing just outside," I said. "You went in very quickly–people do remember that. You were there before the others. You had the time, and you could have put the manuscript into the pile of objects–probably still inside the barrel. Before the technicians got to removing them. It wouldn't have been hard to manage."

"Could have," he said. "I didn't. How can you show otherwise? Don't be silly, boy."

"Well, Sir," I said, "the manuscript wasn't in the barrel before it was unsealed. The isotope assay proves that; it was a modern counterfeit. But it was in the material from the barrel right after that. No one else had an opportunity to add it in–except the technicians themselves."

"Then one of them must have–"

I put up a hand, and it stopped him. "Sir, if First Files Building has to put the three technicians, and yourself, through truth tests–lie-detection apparatus–they'll do it. This is important to them, and the way the government here feels about artifacts they'll get permission to do it."

A long pause. A very long pause.

"This is an impossible position, boy," he said. His voice had slowed and softened. "You can see that."

"Very difficult," I said. "Yes, Sir."

"I found the manuscript in the dig," he said. "Wanted to keep it for myself. You know how a thing like that might be. But I had an attack of conscience. Brought it back, shoved it right in with the things from the barrel. Took a second or so, not difficult. As you said. What's the difference? It all came from the same dig, boy. No harm done, after all."

"It couldn't have happened that way," I said. "Even in the dry atmosphere of the hole, Sir, the manuscript wouldn't have been preserved in the same way–probably not well preserved at all. There would have been differences visible to any examination–and there weren't any."

"Well, there weren't," he said. "And that's the way it happened, boy. An attack of conscience."

I nodded again. "If you say so, Sir," I said, and I went away.

THIRTY-EIGHT

Ten minutes later, I was back on the phone, from my pocket piece—which I had, thank you, remembered to hook into the system before I'd left home. I made two calls, and spoke one word in each—both B'russ'r and the Master knew my voice, and were waiting for the word.

The word was: "Confirmed."

That started the last big set of moves. Now, instead of checking the massive lists of everybody against Ramsay Leake, and everybody against everybody, the two of them could concentrate on checking Gro Rouse against Leake, and against others—a much smaller and simpler job, and one I had some real hopes for.

One small thing bothered me. just a bit. If Rouse had been the shooter, it seemed he'd have to have been the Hell of a good shot: he'd killed exactly once, when he'd meant to. It is easy to kill by accident, and he hadn't done it.

But he hadn't seemed like a marksman to me. There are types of motion you learn to notice—precision and economy, in a way—that signal the real marksman anywhere, and he hadn't shown them. My guess would have been an average shot, maybe a hair better than average, but not spectacular.

Well, Hell, I could be wrong. I finished the calls, and told myself not to worry about it.

Then I went home, where I could sit down in comfort, and called Detective-Major Gross.

"What is this?" he said. "Alibis, now? You want me to go out and track down alibis, Knave? Do you think we're in some sort of 3V crime show, or some such nonsense?"

"I think something will turn up," I said. "He's a careful man, but he'd have had to be in a particular place at a particular time, no way to fudge the time at all—we have Berigot witnesses. If he set up an alibi, it's going to be a tricksy one, and those are—"

"Always the easiest to break down, yes," he said. "I know my trade, you realize." He sighed. "And where did you get this name, now? Divination? A bolt from the bright blue?"

I told him. I never had to mention little Robbin Tress; Gro Rouse's selectively good memory impressed him.

"It's just the sort of detail a man does slip on," he said. "I've seen it a thousand times, you know."

"Welcome to the thousand-and-first," I said, and he said:

"I'll get on this, Knave. It may turn out to be something."

Somehow, I was fairly sure it would.

* * *

AFTER I PUT the phone away, the being I fondly think of as my brain decided it had been cudgeled enough, day after day, and tapped me on the shoulder. It told me to go back and look at an evening I really hadn't enjoyed much at the time, a conversation between two sf fans about social rules. It was very insistent about this, so I went and dug out the files, which I can sometimes find inside my head, and went over them with some care.

After a while, I said: "Oh.. Argon."

It didn't have to be him, of course. There was more than one isotope expert on Ravenal, after all, even if there weren't job lots of them. But the picture was, of course, irresistible. Whoever had actually sat down and written the damn manuscript had to be a Misfit, or someone with equivalent background–and even if there were other underground sf groups on Ravenal (and were there? Would even Mac know, for sure?), what were the chances that a member of one such small minority of people would also be a member of the small minority of isotope experts? The combination looked awfully promising.

It explained, too–and very simply and beautifully–why the forgery had been of a Heinlein manuscript. The man with the technical knowledge also knew a lot about Heinlein; it was, for him, an obvious choice. I'd been wrong about the forger knowing a technical expert: the forger had *been* the technical expert. All right, it was easy to be wrong on that sort of guess, and easy to admit being wrong.

But the basic fact, I realized slowly, was not going to be anything like an easy thing for me to tell the Master about. B'russ'r was fairly familiar with human beings, and he knew that human beings sometimes forgot things, or neglected facts. The Master did not believe this should be so, at least for some human beings.

Me, for instance.

Well, it had to be done, didn't it? I barely gave myself an argument about it, and on the principle of taking the worst first I saved B'russ'r's call for second.

I went for the phone again.

"Who?"

"Gerald Knave again," I said. "There's something else."

"Indeed?"

"There's an expert on isotopes in the picture," I said.

"Some one particular expert?"

I took a deep breath. "He's also a Misfit."

There was a little silence. "Gerald," he said. Sadly.

"Well, I tripped over the fact by accident," I said. "In the course of not listening to two people talk about something else. Corri Reges and Chandes Washington were arguing about etiquette, and he said something about Geraint Beauthis. That's what got me interested—and kept me from hearing much of anything else."

"Gerald," he said again. Even more sadly.

"It seems Chandes Washington was at the library working on something involving isotopes of argon on Kingsley. Long-lived isotopes of argon."

"Unusual," he said. "The data on those isotopes are not yet complete, but do seem convincing. It is perhaps best to keep an open mind on the subject, for the present." And, after another pause: "Gerald, this is not like you."

"It is very like me," I said. "Now and then I screw up. I never added it in—I just let it lie there, and went on."

"Such carelessness," he said, "is the primary reason I worry about you, Gerald. It can result in injury."

Oh, God. "I'll be all right."

"Here in my little home," he said, "alone in the world as I am, an old blind man, and almost helpless, I hear from you very seldom, Gerald. I am afforded much time for worry. For concern. After all, there is little else with which I may occupy my time. Gerald, it is unkind to increase my worries so."

Well, it's no use going through the whole of it for you, and if you don't mind, we'll just chop it off right there. Not at all pleasant—but what else could I have expected? I *had* screwed up, and no screw-up comes without consequences.

I don't mind saying, though, that it shook me. I had a bomb to toss at the Master, and what with one old blind helpless thing and another, I forgot all about it until almost an hour after he'd said, mournfully: "Finished," and I'd put the phone away.

THIRTY-NINE

I DID GET the chance to do it, of course—after a variety of delays. Late the next afternoon, when we finally managed to get together, the four of us. B'russ'r invited us to his tree-house, or nest, or whatever it is the thing should be called. "It will be of interest to note how three people of such varied resources cope with a novel environment," he said by way of explanation.

It was the most awkward disguise for an impulse toward hospitality, I think, I've ever heard—but I let it pass, of course. Personal emotions—and hospitality is a personal emotion—are still novelties for the Berigot (that being perhaps the primary consequence of information upload), and it's going to take some time before they have any real idea how to handle them.

If they do, of course, they'll be one long step ahead of human beings, because God knows we don't.

B'russ'r had provided ladders for us—there's a rental company, Success Ltd., that does very well for itself, with offices near each Berigot colony—and by the time I got there the Master and Robbin had already gone up. I don't suppose Robbin had any difficulty with the ladders—she'd visited Berigot before, I knew—and I am damn sure blind old Master Higsbee didn't. I clambered up myself, and stepped onto the platform, about forty feet in the air.

That's the thing that strikes you first: what there is, is a platform. There are no rooms, no walls, no ceiling, no closed spaces at all. Closed spaces can be arranged at will—the portable-wall shop I'd been in, which seemed the Hell of a long while into the past, probably has more Berigot customers than human ones—but they're for special occasions of one sort or another. The Berigot don't mind weather, in virtually any quantities, and live their lives out of doors.

Objects that weather might damage—and there are fewer of these than you might think; hammocks, tables, desks, chairs (for human visitors) and the like are weather-proofed—used to be guarded by removable canopies, anything from cloth to metal. Now, especially for the more prosperous Berigot (like B'russ'r), the job is done by transparent fields, and a Beri apparently feels more comfortable with everything open and in sight. Theft is not a problem—as the Master had said, the Berigot have a different list of sins.

But canopies are used ceremonially. too. B'russ'r had provided cloth for each of us, on frameworks over three light, but surprisingly comfortable, chairs. Sitting under a brightly colored canopy—these were printed with flower and leaf patterns, bright yellows and blues I took to be Denderus foliage—in the open air gives you an odd feeling that you've suddenly become Royalty, and are about to agree to sign the Magna Carton, or whatever it was. Not at all unpleasant, and luckily it was a fine afternoon.

We were seated in a circle, near one corner of the platform. B'russ'r's sleeping hammock was in another corner, with a small table near it supplied with lights and actual, physical books. His desk, surrounded by rickety-looking but (I'm sure) perfectly solid shelves holding more books, tapes, spools and the like, was in another, and what passes among Berigot for a washroom was established in the fourth. Kitchen arrangements were between hammock and desk.

There was, of course, no stove. Berigot use fire in preparing food about as often as I use a duck press; what they use with constancy is, in fact, a set of what could pass for duck presses. They don't cook their food, or even heat it, more than once a year or so; they press it flat, into a series of mashes, and though they do eat the mashes, they get a great deal of their nourishment from the expressed juices. The kitchen was a large table, with runnels along two sides, many squeeze-bottles, some plates and eating tackle, storage cabinets for food and spices, and an array of presses.

Next to my chair was a tiny table with an ashtray on it. I took the hint, lit up, and offered a cigarette to B'russ'r. He accepted it gracefully, thanked me, and began to chomp away.

"Before we begin," the Master said, "it seems best to refer back to a small difficulty I am sure Gerald has been having."

Hell of an opening. I said: "What difficulty?" and he said:

"Dr. Rouse is not, of course, a marksman. You will have realized this, I hope; you have become neglectful, but surely not neglectful enough to miss such bodily signs as a marksman would provide in any interview."

I took a flier, if the term is allowable on a Berigot platform. "Maybe he didn't fire the shots," I said.

"Economy, Gerald," the Master rasped at me. "We have posited a small group—in all probability three: a ringleader, an isotope expert, and a third party—possibly for the theft itself, as we now begin to assume that the isotope expert was in fact the person who wrote the actual manuscript."

"If he did that," Robbin said, "he must be pretty good as a writer. I mean, even the little bit I heard sounded exciting, and the whole thing sounded like Heinlein to a lot of people who know a lot about sf, I mean."

"It must be a talent of his," the Master said. "He might have used it better."

"To be sure," B'russ'r said. "Counterfeiting a twentieth-century work is a disturbing act; it tampers with the past of your race."

"So it does," the Master said. "And further tampering was planned; we can be deductively sure of that. But it will now not take place; the plan has been intermitted."

"About the marksmanship," I said. "I did see it, thanks—but perhaps we're wrong, and he is that good."

The Master smiled at me. "I remember saying that there was another possibility as regards the shootings," he said. "It is less likely to occur to any of us; we assume purpose in the shootings, because we assume some feeling for the value of life in any person. But let us suppose he simply—did not care one way or the other. Would have been as willing to kill as to miss or maim—and simply accepted the results."

"So I was just lucky?" I said. "Twice?"

"Luckier than you have seen," he said. "You were someone he meant to kill. You might prove dangerous; Ping Boom had undoubtedly spoken of you somewhere, and praised your abilities—no surprise, as he had determined to hire you. The killer tried twice—and after that, with Ramsay Leake dead and a police investigation as well as your own in progress, he did not dare further attempts. He must have needed badly to silence Mr. Leake; once that was done he could only hope you would not succeed. He had missed twice with you, and could not chance a third attempt."

"Oh," I said.

"And perhaps Mr. Leake would have been lucky as well, had he not been at the top of his tower," the Master said. "It is easy to kill by accident;

it is still easier to miss. You were missed twice, though narrowly."

"Damn narrowly," I said.

"Mr. Leake may not have been hit in a vital spot," he said. "The shot did hit him, and he staggered and went over to the ground. It does not matter; vital spot or no, it was murder."

"And the Berigot–"

"Were hit where any shooter could hit them, in the wide wingspan," he said.

"So Rouse just potted away blindly?" I said.

"He wanted to rid the Twentieth wing of three Berigot he felt would be overly careful, or overly suspicious, when a new manuscript came into the wing. He knew them, of course, as he would know any worker in the Twentieth wing, and made his judgments. He cleared the ground; two of them changed assignments, and the third, the youngest and, therefore, least influential of the group, he felt might be left with minimal danger to the plan."

"A horrible plan," B'russ'r said.

"Just so," the Master said. "Lives were damaged. One was taken. And all for eventual monetary profit."

"Money is an awful thing," Robbin said, and the Master turned to her with a gentle smile.

"No, dear girl, money is not terrible. Money is not the root of all evil, and no one but a fool ever said that it was." He paused, and B'russ'r nodded a little sidewise at him. Taking no chances.

The Master shrugged politely, and B'russ'r said: "What your Bible says, in good translation–indeed, in any translation I have encountered–is: The love of money is the root of all evil."

"True," the Master said. "Money is useful. It is an invention of great value. It can express friendship, or love, or simple agreement, or a hundred other things. It can serve as a transfer medium for materials of all kinds. It is not evil. But the love of it–the feeling that it has value of itself, and should be piled up, and admired, and revered–that is an evil, and a great one."

"Money is to buy things with," Robbin said, "if you have to. There are even other ways to get things, a lot of the time–people give them to you because they like you, or because they want to, a lot of reasons. Maybe it's better when you don't need the money part of things, and if you do you just need it, that's all, you don't have to go and do bad things for it."

"Heinlein himself said, over and over," B'russ'r said, "that money problems never exist for a man unafraid of them. There is always an honest way to gain it, he said, if necessary by digging waste pits."

Robbin nodded. "I'd hate that," she said. "But I could do it, if I had to. Maybe in a little while when I'm better, and if I have to, I mean."

I broke in. "Has Gross reported in yet?"

"Not to me," B'russ'r said, and the Master shook his head.

"He would have no reason to call me in preference to one of you," he said.

"Well, that'll come," I said. "About connections, now–"

"It can be established that Dr. Rouse and Dr. Washington had an acquaintance, and a friendly one, six years ago," the Master said.

"Well, that's a first step."

"It can also be established," B'russ'r said, "as far as a negative can be established, that the acquaintanceship–the friendship–stopped very suddenly just over five years ago, and has not been resumed."

"A careful fellow," I said. "Just a hair too careful–that cutoff is a red flag."

"Not the sort of thing to take to a jury," the Master said, "but to the knowledgeable eye, certainly indicative."

"It is a little more indicative than you may assume," B'russ'r told me–carefully not saying anything about the Master's assumptions. Well, he was learning; he'd even asked for permission first, before providing that quote from the Bible. "There exist occasions at which Dr. Rouse's attendance was quite usual, when he was on-planet. Even rigidly fixed; he has been a creature of habit, as it is said–odd to think of habit as having offspring or creations."

"And?"

"And it can be shown that, if such occasions had as an attendee Chandes Washington, during the past five years Dr. Rouse did not attend."

A little too careful, right. And: "You've done the Hell of a lot of work, awfully damn fast, to come up with that," I said.

"It required doing," B'russ'r said. Not a preen–Berigot don't preen. A statement of fact.

Or—just maybe—the beginnings of a preen. Berigot were learning, bit by bit, that there were such things as personal emotions.

What they'd be like in, say, fifty years I had no idea. But it did look to be an interesting fifty years to be around the race.

"Well, it certainly got done," I said. "Damn it, I heard Chandes Washington talking about an isotope search. It was perfectly obvious, and I passed it up."

"Such small slips occur," B'russ'r said gently. "You can scarcely be said to be at fault."

"The truth is," I went on, nodding my thanks at the Beri, "everything about this entire exercise has been obvious."

"I would scarcely say—" B'russ'r began.

"Rouse was obvious," I said. "Most important figure at the dig. A man with a fantastically sizable load of self-importance. Just the type you'd expect to try passing off a counterfeit for a job lot of other people—who, of course couldn't be expected to know better, they weren't Gro Rouse."

"Character alone—" B'russ'r said.

"And a perfect memory for the dig," I said.

B'russ'r nodded. "Indeed."

"I kept being told that a Misfit couldn't have done the job—too much respect for Heinlein—and nobody else could have—not enough background. The answer was obvious: the man without background—Rouse—used a Misfit who had it, Chandes Washington. Who had the technical know-how, too. As for having too much respect—as you were pointing out, Master," I said, "there are people, sad though the fact is, who have much more respect for money than they do for any human being, living or dead."

"Quite so," Master Higsbee said. "It was, of course, his familiarity with Heinlein that made the choice of subject for the forgery simple."

"Familiarity, and contempt," I said. "And the sailplaning was obvious. Damn it, what good is a field that only looks to a height of six feet? Given a nice dark night—which it was, remember, dead of night at that—a bunch of dark sailplane wings, and dark clothing—"

"They had to have the hammock dyed black," Robbin said dreamily. "Hammocks don't come in black. There's a little shop downtown somewhere, and they had it done there."

I blinked. The Master and B'russ'r nodded. All three of us had made the necessary mental note: a dye shop or tailor shop of some sort, downtown. It would not be an impossible job to check that out; a hammock dyed black—a Berigot hammock, I assumed, available anywhere, or any hammock large and strong enough—wouldn't be a job any shop would have been asked to take on every day. The order would turn up in somebody's memory, and on somebody's records.

Silly of them not to do their own dyeing, but Rouse et Cie probably felt it was too small a risk to bother about.

"Given all that, the sailplaning was perfectly obvious," I said. "It just took us a while to see it. And the motive for the whole thing—for everything from the shootings five years ago, through the forgery and theft, to Ramsay Leake the other day—was just as obvious, once you got a straight look at it."

"One thing," the Master said, "was, and remains, less than obvious. Somehow, the thieves passed through that window, without breaking it and without leaving traces. I would have said that, for glassex, that is not a possible occurrence."

I very carefully did not grin. I had set up the conversation hoping that the Master would say something just like that, and by God he had said it.

"That," I said, "is the most obvious part of it all. It's been staring us in the face right from the start. From the first minute I stepped into the Special Exhibits room."

B'russ'r looked politely interested, which is the way a Beri looks when facts he's involved with are about to be supplied.

The Master looked surprised. I had not seen that expression on his square and determined face in something over sixty-one months, and it was worth waiting for.

"Really?" he said, after the briefest of pauses. It had come to him that I'd led him right into this, and he was deciding whether or not to resent it. "From the very first moment?"

"It was the first thing I noticed," I said. "The glass." He opened his mouth, shut it again, sighed briefly, and nodded. B'russ'r said:

"The glass?"

Robbin was looking at me, fascinated. It was the Hell of a story.

"It was glass," I said. "Not glassex. No way to get through glassex—but the whole damn wing is as Twentieth as possible. Old-style locks on the windows. Glass in the windows and on the cases. I saw it. I noticed it—my God, you couldn't help but notice it."

There was a little silence.

"I have seen those windows myself, and several times," B'russ'r said. "Glass. I should have made the connection. I did not." He rustled his wings, sadly. "Now, unbreakable glassex—"

"Can't just be broken—taped first, to avoid bits falling on the floor or down to the ground—and a new pane puttied in. But glass can—if you bring the putty and the pane with you."

"In the hammock," Robbin said breathlessly.

"In the nice dyed hammock we'll be able to trace," I told her.

The Master frowned. "The putty would be new," he said. "Dry by the time anyone saw it, of course, but new. An examination would show that. And nobody would have checked putty on the outside of the damn window, after all—which is where it had to be, or they couldn't have gotten out of the room. They had to put the new glass in from the damn perch, from the outside."

"Like all glassex windows," B'russ'r said. "The locks weren't touched: the pane was most carefully shattered, and then replaced, impossible with glassex."

"And the case—because they could only carry the one pane—"

"Glass being heavier than glassex," the Master put in.

"—showed signs of tampering," I said. "Because there, they did have to get through the locks."

"Perfectly clear," B'russ'r said.

"Obvious, in fact," I said. "And the fact that the damn window *wasn't* glassex was—too damn obvious to see."

FORTY

THE THIRD MEMBER of the party, by God, also turned out to be someone I'd heard of, though not, for a change, someone I'd met. Rouse had managed to talk a Patrol officer in the damn library into helping out with the theft—money, what looked like a very safe way of doing the job, and of course Rouse's influence with the library, to help just a bit in the future career of Ptl. Harra Gleme.

I'd run across the name, I knew, somewhere before—but it took me eight full minutes to remember where. She'd been one of the officers who had notified Geraint Beauthis that his damn catapult was not allowed in the library. She'd also been the young female officer Chandes Washington had said he remembered, vaguely—as being attached to the Twentieth-century wing. He remembered her, all right—he'd robbed the wing with her—and when she'd turned up to notify Geraint Beauthis, he'd mentioned her to me distantly, without even a name. Why not? There was no connection.

It was almost too neat to be believed. But—again—obvious when you thought about it; if you were Rouse, and wanted to pick up a confederate for a fast job that required few brains but a strong back, an officer in the library, right there in the target wing, was your obvious first choice.

That word "obvious" ran through everything like a red thread. Robbin was fascinated by it all—it *had* turned out to be the Hell of a story—and B'russ'r took it all in, filed it in his nervous system, I suppose, and went on with his life.

The Master and I felt like damn fools, but I think he hid it better. I'd surprised him with the business of the glass windows, and he knew perfectly well he had no business being surprised by that, any more than I had any business not seeing the fact for so long. But by the time I left Ravenal he was back to normal—normal for Master Higsbee.

"We have all learned a good deal," he told me in my living room. I'd offered to come to him, but he'd said it was good for him to get out into the world when opportunity offered; an old blind man ran the danger of turning into a recluse, he told me. "This has been a stage in your progress, Gerald, and though it presented you with difficulties you should have overcome more easily—which is of course regrettable—you will in the end be the better for it. You have learned from this experience, I hope. But you must continue learning. And if you find it possible, it would be a kindness to an old and helpless blind man if you could manage somehow to advise me of your progress, or the lack of it, from time to time."

I said I would. Now and then, in fact, when I feel strong enough, I do. "Rouse and Chandes Washington and Harra Gleme will be the worse for it," I said. "They're all guilty of Leake's murder, by Ravenal statutes, and they'll all be living in the Colony a good long while."

"Not a pleasant place," the Master agreed. The Colony is an island near Ravenal's equator—it reminds me of the ancient Devil's Island, a hot, jungle sort of place you couldn't ever leave. Of course, this was Ravenal, so there was a Research Establishment hooked in to the Colony, and the three thieves and murderers and forgers would spend most of their time digging holes, collecting dirt samples, and picking plants. "But they brought it on themselves, Gerald. And the others you know here are recovering well, I understand."

Detective-Major Gross had recovered, at least. He'd taken the bundle of facts we handed him, added in his own check on Rouse's whereabouts at the time of Ramsay Leake's death (there had been an alibi, and even more tricksy than usual, and as brittle as that window glass once Gross got to taking it apart—no need to bother you with the flimsy details), and shuffled it all into a neat pile which he handed off to a City Two official attorney. The trial and conviction had been very rapid, by anybody's standards—Ravenal does go in for efficiency a good deal—and Gross went back to the old stand, investigating one crime or another and cursing citizens, and the occasional tourist. We did get a thank-you from him, though it seemed to pain him a little to deliver it.

The dig people were going about their various businesses, too—Bitsy Bowyer and Paula Shore were set for another Survivalist hole, this one somewhere in a state called Montagne, I think it is, and Dean Rell was in line for Gro Rouse's old spot at the library—pardon me, First Files Building. I wondered what *his* office was going to look like—a lot, I thought, like Paula Shore's. Freda Hocksher, whom I never did get to meet, was still teaching at Lavoisier. Drang Mathias was going about his business, too, and undoubtedly planning to turn into a wheel any week now.

I'd seen rather a lot of Corri Reges, and of course I'd seen Mac. Corri was busy as all Hell—she was getting set to run for President of the Misfits, if Glatz could be levered out, and she rather thought he could.

"People don't like him much," she told me.

"People never like a President much," I said. "In a fan club, it goes with the job. Become President yourself, and people will hate you."

She nodded. "I know," she said in her little viola voice. "But it's a chance to go down in history, Knave. To be part of the roll of Presidents of the Ravenal Misfits. How can I ignore that?"

I nodded. "You can't, of course," I said. "Even if the history is the underground history of an underground sf fan club."

"You never know," Corri said. "Some Moskowitz may be writing it, in secret, right now."

What the Hell, it's possible.

And if some Moskowitz really is writing that history, damn it, I'll be in it, too. I'd seen a lot of Corri Reges, and of Mac too—at Misfit meetings. I'm just another name on the membership lists, but that's something.

I'm kind of proud of it, in fact. Gerald Knave, honorary corresponding member of the Ravenal Misfits. I can't go around boasting about it—there are rules, after all—but just between us, I can mention it here.

Damn proud of it, in fact.

THE END

AUTHOR'S NOTE

There are a few things to be said.

First, of course, it might need to be said—people are touchy just lately—that both Knave and I have more respect and admiration for Robert A. Heinlein than either of us can well say. Nothing said by any person in this report is to be taken as a denigration of himself or his work; indeed, no sf writer mentioned, quoted from, or alluded to by Knave or by any Misfit lacks the respect and admiration we both gladly give him or her. The forgery is of course a forgery and not to be taken as indicative of Heinlein's real, and lasting, work.

Second, special thanks are due, and hereby willingly given, from the author to Jeff Harris, who afforded him the time and space, at great cost, to write the thing—and afforded him much more, as well.

And third, the author's gratitude is most lovingly extended to rebekah, Chatte and jen, for great help with a series of knotty problems early in the work, and to Raven for much help with this and other work.

THE END

Printed in the United States
132248LV00004B/162/A

9 781587 153440